SUGAR CREEK GANG
THOUSAND DOLLAR FISH

Paul Hutchens

MOODY PRESS
CHICAGO

All Scripture quotations are taken from the *New American Standard Bible,* © 1960, 1962, 1963, 1968, 1971, 1972, 1973, 1975, 1977, and 1994 by The Lockman Foundation, La Habra, Calif. Used by permission.

Original Title: *North Woods Manhunt*

ISBN: 0-8024-7019-X

5 7 9 10 8 6 4

Printed in the United States of America

PREFACE

Hi—from a member of the Sugar Creek Gang!

It's just that I don't know which one I am. When I was good, I was Little Jim. When I did bad things—well, sometimes I was Bill Collins or even mischievous Poetry.

You see, I am the daughter of Paul Hutchens, and I spent many an hour listening to him read his manuscript as far as he had written it that particular day. I went along to the north woods of Minnesota, to Colorado, and to the various other places he would go to find something different for the Gang to do.

Now the years have passed—more than fifty, actually. My father is in heaven, but the Gang goes on. All thirty-six books are still in print and now are being updated for today's readers with input from my five children, who also span the decades from the '50s to the '70s.

The real Sugar Creek is in Indiana, and my father and his six brothers were the original Gang. But the idea of the books and their ministry were and are the Lord's. It is He who keeps the Gang going.

PAULINE HUTCHENS WILSON

1

When you just *know* there's going to be some exciting trouble in the next twelve minutes or less, you have to make your red head do some quick clear thinking, if you can.

Not a one of the Sugar Creek Gang knew *what* was going to happen, but the very minute I heard that outboard motor roaring out on the lake, sounding as if it was coming straight toward the shore and the old icehouse we were all in, I said, "Quick, gang! Let's get out of here and get this ransom money back to camp!"

Little Jim's gunnysack had a lot of money in it right that minute, money that we'd dug up out of the sawdust in that abandoned icehouse. The sack was nearly filled with stuffed fish, big and middle-sized northern and walleyed pike with thousands and thousands of dollars sewed up inside.

I won't take time right now to tell you all you maybe ought to know about how we happened to find that ransom money buried in the sawdust of the icehouse. That'd take too long, and, besides, you've probably read all about it in the last story about the Sugar Creek Gang, which is called *The Treasure Hunt.*

I'd better tell you, though, that a little St. Paul girl named Marie Ostberg had been kidnapped and the kidnapper had hidden up in the Chippewa Forest of northern Minnesota in what is called "Paul Bunyan Country," where we were camping. Our gang had found the girl in the middle of the night and then captured the kidnapper in an old Indian cemetery the next night.

Then we had a very mysterious and exciting time hunting for the ransom money in one of the strangest places in all the world to find money. At last we found it in this very old icehouse, sewed up inside these great big fish, which we'd been digging up and stuffing into the gunnysack.

In maybe another seven minutes we'd have had it all dug up and into the sack and would have been on our way back to camp. But all of a startling sudden we heard that outboard motor roaring in our direction. We knew that unless we moved fast we would never be able to get out and far enough away into the bushes not to be seen.

"What's the sense of being scared?" Dragonfly, the pop-eyed member of our gang, asked me right after I'd ordered us all to get going quick. "The kidnapper's caught and in jail, isn't he?"

"Sure, but old hook-nosed John Till's running loose up here somewhere," I said.

John Till was a very fierce man and the unpleasant dad of one of the members of our gang. He had been in jail a lot of times in his wicked life and was staying in a cabin not more than a quarter of a mile up the shore from where we were right that minute.

Poetry, the barrel-shaped member of the gang, who knew 101 poems by heart and was always quoting one, turned around quick, scrambled back across the sawdust we'd been digging in, and peeped through a crack between the logs toward the lake.

"Who is it?" I asked.

And he said in his ducklike, squawky voice, "I can't tell, but he looks awful mad."

Well, anybody knows that nobody could see well enough *that* far to see a person's face and be able to tell whether it had a mad look on it. But if it was John Till, who hated us boys anyway, he probably *would* be mad and would do savage things to all of us if he caught us in that icehouse taking the money.

So we all scrambled as fast as we could out of that icehouse and into the open, carrying Little Jim's gunnysack full of fish. We made a dive across an open space to a clump of bushes, where we wouldn't be seen by anybody on the lake.

Circus, the acrobatic member of our gang, was with us, and he, being the strongest of us, grabbed up the sack, swung it over his shoulder, and loped on ahead.

"Hurry!" we panted to each other and didn't stop running until we reached the top of the hill, which we did just as we heard the outboard motor stop. There we all dropped down on the grass, gasping and panting and happy that we were safe. But I was feeling pretty bad to think that there were probably a half dozen other fish still buried in the sawdust in that old log icehouse.

"Quick, Poetry, give me your knife," Circus ordered.

"What for?" Poetry said and at the same time shoved his hand in his pocket and pulled out his official Boy Scout knife. He handed it over to Circus, who quick opened the heavy cutting blade and started ripping open the sewed-up stomach of the northern pike he'd just pulled out of the sack.

"There's no sense in carrying home a six-pound northern pike with only a quarter of a pound of twenty-dollar bills in it," Circus said.

I knew he was right. It was a long way back to our camp, and if for any reason we had to run fast, we could do it better without having to lug along those great big fish, especially the biggest one.

I didn't bother to watch Circus then, because I started peering through the foliage of some oak undergrowth back toward the lake. And I saw a man come around the corner of the icehouse and stop. The old door hung open, but I could see several boards nailed across the opening on the inside.

"Look!" Dragonfly said. "He's got a big string of fish."

And sure enough he had.

Little Jim, who was beside me, holding onto the stick he always carried with him when we were on a hike or out in the woods, whispered close to my ear, "I'll bet he's got a lot more money sewed up in a lot more fish and is going to bury it in the sawdust where these were."

I happened to have my high-powered binoculars with me, so I quick unsnapped the carrying case they were in. I zipped them out and raised them to my eyes, and right away it seemed I was only about one-third as far away as I really was. I gasped so loud at what I saw— or rather *whom* I saw—that my gasp was almost a yell.

"*Sh!*" Circus said to us, just as if *he* was the leader of our gang, which he wasn't.

I was leader today—that is, I was supposed to be, because our real leader, Big Jim, wasn't with us. He was back at camp with Little Tom Till, the newest member of our gang.

"It's old John Till, all right," I said. I could see his stooped shoulders, dark complexion, red hair, bulgy eyes, bushy eyebrows, and hook nose.

"What if he finds we've dug up part of the fish and run away with them?" Little Jim asked in a half-scared voice.

"Maybe he won't," I said and hoped he wouldn't.

While I was watching John Till toss his stringer of fish into the icehouse and clamber up the boards after them, Circus was slashing open fish and taking out the ransom money, which was folded in nice plastic bags, the kind my mom uses in our kitchen back home at Sugar Creek.

We all helped Circus do what he was doing, all of us maybe more excited than we'd been in a long time, while different ones of us took turns watching what John Till was doing.

I knew that soon he would be out of that icehouse again and probably would go back to the big white boat he'd come to shore in. He'd shove off and row out a few feet, and then there would be a roar of his motor, and away he would go out across the sunlit water, his boat making a long widening V behind him. Then we would sneak back and get the rest of the money.

Everything was now pretty clear in my mind as to what had been going on the last day or two. Perhaps John Till had been what police call an "accomplice" of the real kidnapper, and it had been his special job to look after the ransom money. He'd decided that the best way in the world to hide it where nobody would ever think of finding it would be to catch some big fish, cut them open, clean out the entrails, fold the money in plastic, stuff it inside the fish, and sew them up, the way my mother sews up a chicken she's stuffed with dressing just before she slides it into the oven for our dinner.

Then he would dig down deep in the saw-dust of the icehouse till he came to some ice, lay the fish on it, and cover it up. Nobody would *ever* think to look inside a fish for money. Even if they accidentally dug up a fish, it'd be covered with sticky wet sawdust, and they wouldn't see the stitches in its stomach.

While I was thinking that and also watching the shadow of John Till through the doorway of the icehouse, all of a sudden there was a quick gasp beside me.

I said to Circus, "What on earth?" thinking maybe he'd found something terribly special.

But he hadn't. He dropped his knife, leaped to his feet, and said, "You guys stay here! I'll be right back."

"Stop!" I said. "Where are you going?" I remembered I was supposed to be the leader.

But Circus had his own ideas about that. He squirmed out of my grasp, almost tearing his shirt because I had hold of it and didn't want to let go.

The next second there were only four of us left—barrel-shaped Poetry; kind-faced, great Little Jim; pop-eyed Dragonfly; and me, red-haired, fiery-tempered, freckle-faced Bill Collins. Circus, I saw, was streaking through the bushes as fast as he could go toward the lake and the icehouse but not getting out in the open where John Till could see him.

What on earth? I thought. I didn't dare yell or try to stop him by whistling, or John Till would have heard me. And then who knows what might happen? I didn't have the slightest idea what Circus was up to.

He darted like a scared chipmunk out from some bushes not far from the icehouse and made a dive for the open door.

He's crazy! I thought. *He's going to try to—what* is *he going to try to do?*

I soon found out. It happened so fast that I didn't even have time to think.

Swish! Wham! A half-dozen flying movements and it was all over. Circus grabbed that icehouse door, swung it shut, lifted the big heavy bar and threw it into place, and old hook-nosed John Till was locked inside.

2

Circus no more slammed that icehouse door shut and dropped the heavy bar into place, locking John Till in, than there was a loud pounding and a yelling that sounded as if there was a madman inside.

What to do next was the question. We were an awfully long way from camp, and we five boys certainly weren't big enough to capture him ourselves. Besides, yesterday when we'd first seen him, he'd had a big hunting knife, and who knew but what he might have a gun too? Anybody as fierce and as mad as John Till was right that minute—well, you couldn't tell what he might do if he got a chance.

Circus was coming in our direction now as fast as he could. When a few seconds later he came puffing up to us, he exclaimed, "Come on, gang. Let's run back to camp and get help."

And right that minute I got a bright idea of my own. In fact, it had been swishing around in my mind ever since I'd seen Circus wham that door shut. I said, "Come on, gang. Follow me, and we'll get help in a hurry."

I grabbed up the gunnysack, which had the rest of the stuffed fish in it and the packets of ransom money, and it felt as light as a feather as I started on a dash straight toward the ice-house again.

"Where are you going?" Poetry yelled.

"Back to camp," I said. "Come on!"

"Camp's in the other direction," Dragonfly called after me.

"Do as I say," I yelled back over my shoulder and kept on running like a deer, right for the icehouse.

It felt good to realize that all the gang was following along after me, that I *was* actually the leader—for a while anyway. I had what I thought was a great idea. My dad once told me what happens to a person when he becomes a leader. First, he gets an idea about something that he thinks is wonderful and that ought to be done, and right away he starts getting a lot of people to help him do it.

You see, while Circus was slamming that door and shutting old John Till inside, I was watching with my binoculars. I'd seen John's white boat, which was beached there at the lake, and had noticed that the outboard motor, which was tilted forward in the stern, had a beautiful black shroud on it. I saw it was the same kind our camp director had, and I'd been learning how to run it during the past week. That boat had a powerful motor and could go terribly fast on a lake.

(If there is something I'd rather do than anything else, it is to sit in the stern of a boat, with one hand on the steering handle and, facing the prow, go roaring out across the water with the wind blowing into my freckled face as I watch the shoreline flash by.)

I also knew that the water in many of the big blue-water lakes up here in the north woods was kept fresh because the Mississippi River flowed through them, flowing from one lake to another. I'd studied a map of the territory and knew that, if we could use that boat, we could go roaring up the lake terribly fast, pass the old Indian cemetery in three or four minutes, and a little later come to a place where the Mississippi flowed out of this lake into a long narrow channel into the lake on which we had our tents pitched. Once we got into that other lake, we'd race up the shore and get back to camp in less than half the time it would take us to hike through the woods carrying a heavy sack of fish.

We could leave John Till locked up in the icehouse while we were gone and hurry back with Big Jim and maybe some other help. Before long we'd have John Till *really* captured. After that, we'd tell the police what we'd done, and then we could claim the reward for finding the thousands and thousands of dollars that the little Ostberg girl's dad had paid to the kidnapper.

In a minute I was hurrying past the icehouse with my gunnysack of fish. I stopped just for a second to listen, but everything was pretty quiet. I noticed that the heavy door was really strong, and I didn't see any way John Till could get out. There also was only one place where he could even *see* out, and that was through a crack on the side next to the lake.

And then all of us were in the boat, had shoved off, and were rowing out to deep enough water to make it safe to start the motor without its propeller striking on the bottom. It was a pretty sunshiny day, with only a few scattered white clouds in the sky.

I was pretty nervous and scared and also brave at the same time. It wasn't our boat or our motor, but we weren't *stealing* it. We were amateur detectives using the criminal's boat to get some help to capture him.

In another minute we'd be gone. Poetry sat in the middle on a seat by himself, Dragonfly and Little Jim were in the one right in front of me, and Circus had a narrow seat up in the prow.

"I don't see why you don't let me run it," Poetry complained. "After all, I taught you how to run it in the first place."

"*Sh!*" I said. "Can't you cooperate?" That is a word my dad sometimes uses when he wants me to obey him. "You keep your eye on the gunnysack there between your feet."

I quick opened the gasoline shutoff valve as far as it would turn, being sure first that the air vent on the tank was open. Then I shoved the speed control lever over to where it said "Start," primed the motor, and gave the starter knob a fast sharp pull. John Till's powerful motor roared itself to life, and the boat started whizzing up the lake. I made a couple of other quick adjustments, and away we went, the wind blowing hard in our faces or against our backs, depending on which direction we were facing.

Circus yelled over the tops of the other kids' heads to me and said, "Hey, Bill. He's yelling and screaming for us to stop."

"Let him yell," I said. "We'll give him something to yell about a little later." I shoved the speed control lever to the right, and our boat really shot forward, Circus's prow raised itself partway out of the water, and we went flying up the shore at a terrific rate of speed.

It had been a wonderful vacation for all of us, I thought, and yet we still had a half-dozen days before we would get into the station wagon and drive the long day and a half back to Sugar Creek. We'd had a lot of fun fishing and swimming and solving mysteries, such as finding a kidnapped little girl, capturing the kidnapper, and digging up the ransom money —a lot of which was right there in the boat with us, some still in the stomachs of the fish in the gunnysack. The rest of the money was probably all sewed into the other fish that John Till had with him right that minute while he was locked up in that icehouse jail. Of course, we still had to actually capture him.

Thinking that, I said to Poetry as he sat grinning in front of me—one of his pudgy hands holding onto the gunwale on each side —"I'll bet Big Jim'll want to call the police and let *them* capture John."

Not a one of us liked that idea very well,

and we all said so, although we'd all had enough dangerous experiences for one vacation.

It was Little Jim's newest hobby that helped make this last story of our northern camping trip one we'd never forget as long as we lived.

And this is the way his hobby got mixed up with our mystery. Our boat had just rounded a bend and was about to swish past the old Indian cemetery where we'd had so many exciting experiences and—as you maybe know—where we'd caught the kidnapper himself one spooky night, when all of a sudden Little Jim yelled, "Hey, gang, there's a whiskey bottle floating out there in the water. Let's stop and get it."

He pointed toward the shore where the cemetery was, and there *was* what looked like a whiskey bottle floating on the surface.

"We don't have time to stop," I yelled to Little Jim and didn't bother to throttle the motor even a little bit. But when I saw that little guy's happy face suddenly get a sad expression on it and saw him drop his head the way a friendly dog does when you scold it, I felt sorry for him and decided that maybe seventeen seconds' lost time wouldn't make any difference. So I shoved the speed control lever to "Slow" and shoved the steering handle around so that we'd cut a wide circle, and then we were putt-putting slowly back toward the floating bottle.

You see, all the members of the Sugar Creek Gang were almost as interested in Little Jim's new hobby as he was. For about a week he'd been collecting all the old empty whiskey bottles he could find. Being an honest-to-goodness Christian boy who hated whiskey because it was a terrible enemy of mankind and made so many people in the world sad and caused so much trouble, he had been putting gospel tracts in the bottles with a little note, which he scribbled in his own handwriting.

A gospel tract, just in case you might never have heard of one, is a little folder with a printed message on it telling whoever reads it something important out of the Bible, especially how to be saved and become a Christian.

The kind of awkward scribble that Little Jim tucked into each bottle along with the tract always said the same thing, which was: "Whoever finds this, please believe that God loves you. If you're not saved, remember Jesus died on the cross for you and wants you to pray to Him and thank Him for doing it and give your heart to Him *quick*. If you don't know how to do it, send me your name and address, and I'll send you a free book telling you how."

Little Jim would sign his name, Jim Foote. He also gave his Sugar Creek address. Then he'd cork up the bottle good and tight and toss it out into the lake for somebody to find and read.

We'd all been having fun helping him, and we could hardly wait till we got back home to Sugar Creek to see if Little Jim had any mail from anybody who had found one of his notes.

You see, Little Jim had his mind made up that sometime, when he was grown up, he was going to be a missionary, but he couldn't wait that long to be one so he was trying to be one *now*. Since he was a great guy and also one of my best friends, I had decided I wasn't going to wait till I was any more grown up than I was before doing it too.

Our boat was gliding slowly up alongside the bobbing bottle, and Circus, who was closer to it than Little Jim, reached out his hand and caught hold of it and started to hand it over to Little Jim. Then he let out a yell and said, "Hey, it's got something tied to it!"

I saw it had. There was a piece of heavy fishing line tied around the bottle's neck, and something was fastened to the other end away down in the water somewhere.

3

The very second I realized there was something tied to the other end of that fishing line, I was afraid it might be some heavy object. And at the rate our boat was traveling, if Circus held onto the bottle, the line might break.

So I yelled to him, "Let go! The line might break!" At the same time, I quick shut down the gas to almost nothing and swung the boat around in a half circle. In case Circus *didn't* let go, the line wouldn't have too much strain on it and break. I was wondering what on earth might be on the other end.

The motor made a couple of smoky coughs and stopped, which was maybe a good thing because we *might* have broken the line if it hadn't.

You could have knocked me over with a pine needle when we found there was already a message in that bottle. There wasn't anything on the other end of the very strong fishing line except an old-fashioned horseshoe. It was covered with weeds and lake-bottom dirt, which meant it had been used as a weight so that the waves wouldn't wash the bottle away.

It took us only seconds to read what was in the bottle, because we didn't even have to take out the cork. A piece of paper with black printing on it was rolled up inside, with the words as plain as anything visible right through the glass. Poetry read them out loud to us in his squawky voice:

Dear Fisherman Friend:
This is one of the best places on the lake for crappie fishing. Try it here Monday through Saturday an hour before and after sundown. But on Sunday at 11:00 and 7:30, come to THE CHURCH OF THE CROSS, Bemidji, Minnesota, where we are fishing for men. We will be pleased to welcome you. Please leave this marker here for others to read. And remember that Christ Jesus came into the world to save sinners, which means you, me, and anybody else.

The Pastor

P.S. Tune in THE CHURCH OF THE CROSS radio broadcast every afternoon at 4:00.

Well, our boat was maybe only a few yards from where we'd first seen the bottle floating, not far from the shore and just straight out from the old Indian cemetery. So we took the oars, which every motorboat ought to have in it, and rowed a few strokes back to where we thought the bottle had been floating before.

Poetry was about to put it carefully back into the water when Dragonfly piped up and said, "Let's tie some *other* weight on it. I'd like to keep that horseshoe for good luck."

"You're crazy," Poetry squawked. "That'd be stealing, and stealing would mean *bad* luck."

Just that second there was a long high-pitched quavering cry of a loon from somewhere on the lake, and Dragonfly—who'd been having a hard time getting used to a loon's lonely cry—looked up quick as though he had heard a ghost.

At the same time, Circus let the horseshoe sink into the lake. A second later, there was the bottle floating on the surface of the water again, lying flat, which meant that the horseshoe was really on the bottom and the line was loose.

Right away, I adjusted the motor for starting, gave a sharp pull on the starter knob, and away we went again, racing up the shore toward The Narrows, where we knew the river flowed from this lake into the one our campsite was on. In another ten minutes, we'd be there, and Big Jim would help us decide what to do about John Till.

It was a wonderful ride, and if we hadn't been so excited, we would have enjoyed the scenery as we had once before when we were riding through The Narrows. The Narrows were almost a half mile long, and there was a little current. But the river was flowing in the same direction we were going, so in only a few minutes we were on our own lake, and the pretty black-shrouded motor was carrying us fast straight for camp.

Poetry yelled, "Remember yesterday afternoon when it rained, and we were in old John's cabin, and we found that little radio, and when we turned it on, we heard a Christian program? I'll bet that was The Church of the Cross program."

Then Little Jim, who was sitting beside Dragonfly with one hand holding his stick and the other the side of the boat, said with a grin on his face, "Radio's a good way to fish for men. It's like casting with a terribly long line clear out where the fish really are."

"Old John Till's a *fish*, all right," Dragonfly said. "Only he drinks whiskey instead of water. I hope when we get him captured, he'll have to go to jail the rest of his life."

I noticed that Circus's monkey-looking face had a very serious expression on it for a minute, as if what Dragonfly had said had been like a pin sticking him somewhere. I remembered that Circus's dad had once been an alcoholic himself.

Even while we were racing along with the oak and white birch and balm of Gilead and pine trees whizzing past, as our boat cut a fierce, fast V through the water, I was remembering that summer night back at Sugar Creek when there'd been a big tent filled with people and a choir and an evangelist preaching. Nearly all of the members of the Sugar Creek Gang had already been saved.

And when Circus himself walked down the grassy aisle to the front to confess the Savior, all of a sudden old Dan Browne, Circus's drinking dad, who had been outside the tent listening, had come rushing in. He ran down the aisle with tears in his eyes and voice, crying, "That's my boy! That's my boy!" And that very night God had saved old Dan Browne clear through, so that he hadn't taken a drop of whiskey or beer since. From then on he was a good worker, and his family had had enough to eat.

Circus must have been thinking the same thing, because when Dragonfly said that about hook-nosed John Till's going to jail, he looked across the top of all the heads of the rest of the gang and straight into my eyes. I could see the muscles of his jaw working as though he was thinking hard. I also noticed that his fists were doubled up terribly tight, and I remembered that he hated whiskey worse than anything else in the world, because it had made his mother very unhappy for a long time.

Little Jim called out to all of us then and said, "What about *Tom?* What'll we tell *him?*"

And what will *we tell him?* I thought—that neat little redhead who was the newest member of our gang and was old John Till's boy.

Not a one of us knew. But in a little while now, at the rate we were flying, we'd be back in camp where Big Jim and Little Tom Till were. And we'd have to tell them that we had Tom's dad locked up in the icehouse and that he was probably what police called an accomplice of the actual kidnapper we'd caught last week.

Big Jim heard our motor and came out to the end of the long dock where the mailbox was to meet us, probably wondering who on earth we were at first, coming in with a different boat.

It turned out that Little Tom wasn't in camp right then but was up the shore visiting at a cabin owned by a man named Santa, who especially liked him. Tom was watching him build a utility boat in his workshop, so we had a chance to tell Big Jim the whole exciting story without Tom's hearing it.

We didn't *want* Tom to hear it, as he would start feeling terribly sad and have all the rest of his vacation spoiled—although, of course, he'd *have* to find it out sooner or later.

"Let's leave Tom where he is and all of us go back with a rope and tie him up," Dragonfly suggested.

"You're crazy," Circus said. "He might have a gun and might shoot us and get away and take all the rest of the ransom money with him."

"What ransom money?" Big Jim wanted to know, and then I remembered that he didn't know a thing about our digging in the old icehouse and finding the money sewed up inside a lot of fish's stomachs. So we quickly told him.

He frowned at first. Then his bright mind started to work, and he just took charge of things. But I was terribly disappointed at what Big Jim decided to do.

"This is a job for the police," he told us. "You boys have done your part, and you'll get credit, but there isn't any sense in running any unnecessary risks. Let's get to a phone quick."

We all knew there wasn't any sense in trying to argue Big Jim out of that idea, and it did make good sense, although it's hard on a boy to use good sense all the time, on account of his not being used to it.

The first good sense we used was to quick carry the money down to Santa's cabin and lock it up in his boathouse. Since the nearest telephone was farther up the lake at a resort, Santa and Big Jim took Santa's boat and motored terribly fast in that direction, leaving Poetry and Circus and Little Jim and Dragonfly and Tom Till—who had just come back—and me standing there by the boathouse to wait till they returned from phoning the police.

I looked into Poetry's bluish eyes, and he into mine. We both felt pretty sad.

It was going to be a *little* fun watching the police surround the icehouse, though, and seeing them capture our criminal.

"It'll be fun to watch him come out of that icehouse with his long hairy arms up in the air," Dragonfly said.

Little Tom looked up from what he'd been doing, which was tucking the stem of an oxeye daisy through the buttonhole of his shirt. That little guy always liked to wear a wildflower of some kind. He asked, "Watch *who* come out of an icehouse—*what* icehouse?"

And Dragonfly, not thinking but letting the very first thought that came into his head just splash right out of his mouth, said, "Why, old hook-nosed John—"

But that was as far as his dumb sentence got. Circus, who was quicker than a cat, whirled around and clapped his hand over his mouth just in time to stop him at the word "John."

But it was too late to save Little Tom's feelings. I saw a sad look come into his blue eyes and both fists double up quick, and I knew he was both sad and mad. He knew Dragonfly meant his dad, because he had called him "old hook-nosed John," but the part about coming out of an icehouse with his hairy arms up in the air must have puzzled him.

I saw him swallow hard, as if there was a lump in his throat, and he said, "You mean my dad's locked up somewhere? What for? What's he done?"

I'd been calling John Till "old Hook-nose" myself when I'd been talking to the rest of the gang and thought about him, but somehow right that second it sort of seemed we ought to get a more respectable, better-sounding name for him.

I knew we had to tell Tom the truth, since he'd heard Dragonfly say that, but I was mad at Dragonfly for a minute. I said, "Listen, you, Dragonfly Gilbert, you can stop calling him 'old Hook-nose,' when you've got a nose that turns south at the end yourself!"

Then, because Tom would have to know the truth sometime, all of us helped each other tell him the whole story, which you already know.

While we were doing it, Tom wouldn't look us in the eye but was picking blue flowers and tucking them into a little bouquet in his hand. Then he straightened up and looked all around in a quick circle as if he was expecting to see the police coming. Also, he looked out toward the lake. He seemed to be listening for Santa and Big Jim's boat coming back.

There wasn't any motorboat sound, but at that very second I heard the sad sound of a mourning dove from up in a tree somewhere, saying, *"Coo, coo, coo, coo."* Then almost the second the last *"coo"* was finished, there was a sort of vibrating sound about thirty feet above us, and I knew it was the wings of the dove as it flew away or maybe flew from one tree to another.

Little Jim had my binoculars. He put them up to his eyes and looked, just as red-haired Tom Till said, "If my dad gets caught, he'll have to go to jail for a terribly long time, and we won't have any dad, and it'll break my mother's—"

He suddenly broke off what he was saying and got a tearful expression on his freckled face. Then, I guess because he couldn't stand to have any of us see him cry, he turned like a flash and started running back toward camp as fast as he could go, stumbling awkwardly as though he had a lot of tears in his eyes that were blinding him and he couldn't see where he was going.

4

Well, when you see one of your best friends running and stumbling along like that and know there are tears in his eyes and that he has a great big heavy ache in his heart, you sort of get tears in your eyes yourself.

All in a flash, while his red hair was bobbing down that weed-grown path toward camp, I was remembering the first time I'd ever seen him. He and his bad big brother, Bob, belonged to a gang of tough town boys that had come out in the country one afternoon and had been eating up all the strawberries that grew on Strawberry Hill. Our gang happened onto them while they were doing it, and for some reason we'd gotten into a fierce fistfight. Tom's hard-knuckled fist had whammed me on the nose, and for a dozen fist-flying minutes he and I had been enemies.

But a lot of things had happened after that. Tom and I made up, and he was now one of the best friends I had. The whole gang liked him a lot, and we didn't hold it against him that his big brother was what people called a "juvenile delinquent" and his dad was a beer and whiskey drinker who acted as though he hated God and the church and was too lazy to work for a living.

So when I saw Tom go stumbling away like that, I got a big lump in my throat and started off after him—not too fast though, because I didn't think he wanted anybody to follow him.

When I got to camp, I heard Tom inside our director's tent, moving around doing something. I couldn't guess what.

It seemed I was sort of spying on him, and I hated to make him feel worse by looking at his tears, if he was still crying. So I slipped into the other tent and peeped through the nearly closed flap. All of a sudden I saw Tom thrust open the flap of his tent real quick, dive out and around it, and start on the run up the lake in the other direction, carrying his small old-looking brown suitcase. And I wondered, *What on earth?*

I was so surprised for a minute that I couldn't even move, and it wasn't until after Tom disappeared down the path, running as fast as he could with that suitcase flopping along beside him, that I realized he was probably so ashamed he was going to try to run away and go back home.

Then I came to life, dived out of my tent, and started after him, yelling, "Hey! Tom! Wait for me! I want to tell you something."

I didn't know what I wanted to tell him, but if he would only wait till I got there, I could probably think of something. I certainly didn't want him to go home.

Behind me I could hear the sound of Santa's motorboat on the lake and—well, I darted after Tom Till as fast as my excited legs could carry me.

I was a little longer-legged than Tom and caught up with him after only a short run. I grabbed him and said, "You're a great guy, Tom. The whole gang likes you."

He dropped his suitcase, pulled loose, and scurried around behind the big bole of a Norway pine tree, where he stopped.

I could see part of him and could tell by the way one of his elbows was moving that he was wiping tears out of his eyes, maybe with the back of his hand.

I tried to coax him to go back to camp with me, but he wouldn't.

"Everybody hates me," he sobbed. But he knew I really liked him, as I had proved that to him at different times.

He slumped down in the grass and let himself sort of sob and sniffle and talk at the same time. He wasn't looking at me but straight ahead in the direction of a little cluster of bright yellow mustard flowers, the kind that grow along the edge of our garden back at Sugar Creek if you let them. They are very pretty but are pests, and if you give them a chance they will spread in a few years all over a field or fencerow.

Seeing those pretty mustard flowers and knowing that Tom was crying on account of his dad and also on account of his mother, I thought of my own parents and how when I catch a cold, my brown-haired mom makes a mustard plaster and puts it on my chest.

"You're a super guy," I said to Tom and felt awfully warm inside my heart toward him. I wished he was my brother and that I could do something to make him happy.

Tom seemed to remember then that he had a handkerchief in his pocket. He pulled it out and blew his freckled nose. Then he straightened up quick as if he'd thought of something important. "Where *is* the icehouse?" he asked and scrambled to his feet.

I wondered what he had on his mind, because his face looked as though he'd made up his mind to do something terribly important, which he was afraid to do but was going to do anyway.

But he wouldn't tell me until I said I wouldn't show him where the icehouse was if he *didn't* tell me. So he told me. Would you believe this? This is what he said: "I want to get there before the cops do and talk to him about something. I want to *tell* him something."

I looked at his tearful eyes and his sniffling nose and his freckled face and liked him even better than ever. Then I decided we ought to ask Big Jim what *he* thought, as he had a lot of bright ideas about things like that.

Right away we found Big Jim, who had just come back with Santa from phoning the police, and I was surprised when he said, "Nothing doing. It's up to the police now."

But Tom got a stubborn expression on his

face and said, "I've *got* to talk to him. You've *got* to take me there, because after the cops get him I won't have any chance."

We were standing down on the beach at the time. Tom's bare toes were digging themselves into the sand, and he was still sniffling a little and swallowing. "I want to ask him to give up when the police come for him," he said.

"You won't need to ask him *that*," Dragonfly, who had come up just that second, said. "He'll *have* to give up."

"He might not," Tom said. "He might kill some of the police—he might even kill himself—if he's—if he's been drinking. My dad's pretty fierce when he's half drunk and mad at the same time."

I looked at Big Jim's face.

He was looking down at the boat with the black-shrouded outboard motor attached to the stern, and the muscles of his jaw were working as they do when he's thinking. Barry, our camp director, hadn't come back yet—he had to be away all night—so Big Jim was still our boss.

"Is that your dad's motorboat?" Big Jim asked Tom Till, pointing toward it.

Tom said, "I don't know. He always wanted one like that, but I don't think he had enough —*sniff—sniff*—money to buy one."

Just that second we heard a horn blowing out on the lake. We knew it was the mail boat coming, and we soon learned it had brought letters for most of us. One was addressed to Little Tom Till in his mother's handwriting.

Tom held it in his hands, studying it. Then he opened it and read it, while different ones of us read our own letters. But I kept watching him out of the corner of my eye. Then I saw him quickly shuffle over to Big Jim and shove the letter into his hand and say, "Read *that!*"

Big Jim had been reading a letter written in a very smooth, pretty handwriting in green ink. I knew it was from Sylvia, whose pop was our Sugar Creek minister and who Big Jim thought was extra nice. Jim tucked Sylvia's letter inside his shirt pocket and read Tom's mom's letter and—well, whatever it said, that was what decided him.

"All right, gang," Big Jim said in a quick, authoritative voice, when he'd finished Tom's letter. "Let's get going. We've got to get this letter to John Till before the police get there. Circus, you and Dragonfly run down to the boathouse and wait with Santa. That icehouse is on some new lakefront property he bought two weeks ago, and he'll show the police how to get there."

"I want to go with you," Dragonfly whined.

"You can come with the police, if they'll let you," Big Jim said. "They'll be here as quick as they can."

So Big Jim, Tom Till, Little Jim, Poetry, and I got into John Till's boat, and I let Big Jim run it because he was going to anyway.

First, we checked to see if we had enough gas, and we tossed in enough life preserver pillows for each of us. Little Jim put on his vest just to be still safer, and in a few jiffies we were off. Big Jim ran the boat almost as well as I could, and I only had to tell him once what to do, but he had already done it.

I won't take time to tell you much about that fast ride, but we flew up the lake, through The Narrows, under the bridge, and into the other lake in what seemed only a few minutes.

Just after we'd roared under the bridge and out into the lake the icehouse was on, Little Jim yelled, "There's a long black car just going across the bridge now. I'll bet that's the police."

I couldn't hear the boards of the bridge or the car's engine because our boat was making so much noise. But it felt good to be working with the police, and it also felt good to know there were really a lot of big strong men in our country who were interested in doing what Dad calls "protecting society from wicked men." Only, with Little Tom there in the boat beside me, he being such a super guy, it seemed too bad to think of his dad as a criminal, but he was anyway!

Even while we raced up the other shore past the Indian cemetery and the whiskey bottle, which I noticed was still there—the one that had the printed gospel message in it—I couldn't help but wonder if maybe nearly every criminal in the world had some relative such as a brother or a sister or maybe a wife or a boy or girl who felt as Tom was feeling right then. He looked awfully sad. For some reason it seemed that maybe it was also a big crime to hurt people's hearts the way Tom's was being hurt right that second.

I sort of let my mind fly away like a balloon in the sky for a minute. What if John Till was *my* dad, and I was on my way to an old ice-house, where he was locked up, to give him a letter from my neat brown-haired mom? And what if in twenty minutes maybe he would be arrested for being an accomplice in a kidnapping and might not only have to go to jail for life but might even have to have what is called "capital punishment"—which is being electrocuted or hanged?

Little Jim piped up with a question then that burst my balloon and brought me down to earth. It was, "How'll we get the letter to your dad? We don't dare open the door."

Poetry's bright mind thought of a way. He said, "We'll make a ladder out of ourselves and push Tom up, so he can poke the letter through the crack between the logs." That was a good idea.

A little later, we rounded a bend in the lake, and Big Jim steered straight toward the beach in front of the old log icehouse, where we'd left John Till a little less than an hour before. My heart was pounding fast and hard. I was feeling tense inside on account of Tom, wondering what was in the letter and also what Tom wanted to tell his pop.

Big Jim shut off the motor at just the right speed, and we glided up to the shore. After beaching the boat and tossing the anchor onto the sand, we scrambled out and sneaked up close to the icehouse.

We moved quietly so we wouldn't be heard, although John Till would have heard our motor when we were coming in, I supposed.

"*Sh!*" Big Jim said to us.

He and Tom led the way as we crept closer. I didn't know what would happen next, but I soon found out.

Big Jim stopped the rest of us and sent Tom on toward the icehouse alone.

I peered through the leaves of the wild chokecherry shrubs we were crouching be-hind. Then I heard Tom's pathetic voice that had a kind of a quaver in it as though he was scared, calling out, "Dad!"

We listened for an answer but couldn't hear any.

Then Tom's voice called again, a little louder, close to the side of the log house.

I had both hands up to my ears, listening, but there wasn't a sound, except right that second I heard a very pretty wren's song. It sounded half like a fast mixed-up whistling tune and half like the springwater that trickles out of the rocks not far from the old swimming hole back at Sugar Creek.

Then Tom called still louder, "*Dad!* It's *me* —Tom! I've got a letter for you from Mother!"

But that icehouse was as quiet as if it had been an extralarge grave house in an Indian cemetery.

Tom turned around then and looked in our direction with a question mark on his face.

All of us came out into the open and went toward him, not knowing what to think. In a little while the police would be there, and it'd be too late for Tom to tell his dad what he wanted to tell him or to give him the letter or anything. And then I heard a motorboat coming from somewhere and wondered if it might be Santa's big boat, bringing the police and Circus and Dragonfly.

Poetry—who had been with me the night before when we'd seen John Till taking a string of fish down to the lake from his cottage—whispered, "Maybe he was so tired he went to sleep. Let's all go up and surround the icehouse and yell him awake."

We decided that might be a good idea, so we hurried toward Tom Till. Poetry and I hustled around to the side where the door was.

Well, you could have knocked me over with a puff of wind. There in front of my astonished eyes was that great big icehouse door, wide open on its rusty hinges. *Our prisoner had escaped!*

5

Well, that was that, and it was terribly disappointing. Poetry and I stood staring at that open door, wondering what had happened. Who had opened it and let John Till out, and where had he gone? Was he hiding somewhere close by, and might he spring from behind something any minute and knock the living daylights out of one of us?

Big Jim and the rest of the gang came running around to where we were, and as soon as we found that our prisoner was *really* gone, we looked at each other with sad and disappointed eyes.

I looked at Tom, who had his mom's letter in his hands, and I noticed it was all crinkled, the way letters get when you squish them up tight.

"What'll we do?" different ones of us asked the rest of us, and we waited for Big Jim to decide what.

He looked at Tom, who looked sad and surprised and disappointed. For a second it seemed he didn't belong to our gang at all but was a strange boy—like a lost duckling that gets hatched with a nestful of fluffy little chickens and follows the mother hen around with the chickens but doesn't do what they do or look like they look.

"We've got to find my dad!" Tom said. He stooped down and picked a small white five-petaled flower growing beside the icehouse on a little plant five or six inches high. The plant had shining green three-sectioned leaves with little notches in them.

Little Jim saw him pick it and stooped quickly and picked one himself, saying, "It's a goldthread flower. Goody!"—which goes to show that even in an exciting time that little guy can be interested in something else.

I remembered that he had a flower guide-book. Besides having a hobby of putting a gospel message in whiskey bottles, he was also trying, while we were on our vacation, to find as many wildflowers as he could. He wrote their names in a notebook to show to our teacher that fall when school started.

Tom seemed to be thinking. He didn't say more to Big Jim but looked down at his gold-thread and at the crinkled-up letter in his hand and then began to try to push the goldthread stem through the button in his shirt beside the oxeye daisy that was still there.

I won't have room at this part of the story to tell you what happened when the police came, which they did pretty quick, except to say that as soon as they believed that we hadn't let John Till out ourselves, they dug around in the ice-house and found a lot of other fish with part of the ransom money in them—enough, when they added what *we* had locked up in Santa's boathouse, to make more than $20,000.

But where was the rest of the money? Nobody knew, and nobody knew where John Till had disappeared to. He wasn't in the old cabin we'd once seen him in, which we found he'd rented from Santa. Both the cabin and the icehouse belonged to Santa, who had bought them from a real estate man only a few weeks before.

It was awfully hard on Tom to know that even though his dad was free, the police were still after him, and nobody knew when he'd be caught, or whether he'd try to resist arrest and be shot and maybe killed.

Another thing that made it hard for Tom was the letter from his mother, which he let me see. When I read it, I couldn't blame Tom for feeling sad.

Part of the letter said,

I think maybe your father is up in the north woods somewhere where you boys are camping, Tom. I don't know for sure. But we got a notice from the bank that the interest on our loan is past due, and it has to be paid. If he stops in to visit you, please give him this letter.

As you know, I gave him the egg money I'd saved up all winter and summer, and he was going to take it to the bank just before he left. I'm sure he went fishing, because his tackle is gone.

But don't worry, Tommy boy, we'll get along somehow. The Lord is on our side. You just keep on having good boyish fun and learning all you can in the evening campfire Bible lessons. You and I will keep on praying for your dad and your brother, Bob, that someday they'll both be saved. Our minister called this morning, and he's praying too. And he says God can do things nobody thinks He can . . .

There was more in Tom's letter from home. His white rabbit had carrots for breakfast and seemed quite content but was probably lonesome for Tom. And the new potatoes in the garden would make awfully good raw-fried potatoes for supper when he came home.

It really was a nice letter—the same kind I got from *my* mom, with scribbling all around the edges, things for a boy to remember not to do and why. Don't catch cold, and be careful not to fall out of the boat, things like that, which always worry a mother, who can't help it, because she is a mother.

We kept on the lookout for John Till every minute of that day and the next, when we took a trip to the headwaters of the Mississippi. Little Jim took notes on that trip so he could show them to our teacher that fall when we got back to Sugar Creek. One of his notes said:

The Mississippi River is 2,470 miles long from the place where it starts at Itasca

Lake, Minnesota, to where it stops at the Gulf of Mexico.

We started out early in the morning in our station wagon for Itasca State Park, where there was a big blue-water lake that is eight miles around. There, in a pretty, shady park, all of us scrambled out and followed each other along a little winding path till we came to the lake.

There we saw a small stream of water about twelve feet across and a foot or less deep flowing out of it, making a very pretty noise, which sounded like half a sigh and half a ripple. The sound was also mixed up with the voices of different birds, which were singing all around and above us in the bushes and trees.

We all were quiet for a while, not seeing what we had expected to see when we saw the source of the Mississippi River, but it was very interesting anyway.

Little Jim got a mischievous twinkle in his eyes. Then he quick stooped down and in a jiffy had both his shoes and socks off. I knew he was going to wade across the stream, which was shallow and narrow there. Right away we all had our shoes and socks off, and every single one of us waded across the Mississippi River.

"Here we are," I said, as most of us stopped out in the middle of the Mississippi and gathered ourselves into a half circle with our faces looking toward shore, where our camp director had a camera waiting to take our picture.

Standing there, squinting in the direction

of the camera and also in the direction of the sun, I happened to remember a brand-new Paul Bunyan story that Poetry had made up once, and which you maybe know about if you've read *Screams in the Night*. Old Babe, which is Paul Bunyan's blue ox, was swimming in the headwaters of the Mississippi, and the blue began to come off and make the water blue. And because the Mississippi flows through a lot of the lakes in Minnesota, pretty soon all the lakes became what are called blue-water lakes.

Of course, it was only a legend. Paul Bunyan, as you know, was a pretend lumberman who was extra large; and Babe, the blue ox, was his best friend and went everywhere he went, just as a boy's dog follows a boy around.

Anyway, while we were having our picture taken, I remembered the story Poetry told about how the lakes got their blue water. So I looked down quick at Poetry's large feet and at all the seventy different-shaped and different-length toes on the fourteen feet of all seven of us. I tried to think of something funny to say, but it really wasn't as funny as I thought it would be. "If all the fish in the lakes up here get terribly sick and die before long, it'll be because the barrel-shaped boy in our gang didn't wash his feet before he waded across the Mississippi River."

And that's how it happened that I wished I had brought along a change of clothes, because for some reason what I said made Poetry mad.

He shoved his shoulder against me, and—because I was standing in fast-flowing water halfway up to my knees anyway—when I stepped sideways to try to get my balance, I stepped on a slippery rock in the riverbed and lost my whole balance. The next thing I knew I was sitting down on the bottom of the Mississippi River, and the water was coming clear up to my stomach.

Right away Barry pointed his camera in our direction and took another picture.

That reminded Poetry of a riddle, which he quick asked. It was: "Say, gang, what is it that stays in bed all day, spends all its time at the bank, and never stops running?"

"A river," Dragonfly said and sneezed twice, because he is not only allergic to different pollens but to sudden changes of temperature. The water in that little narrow babbling stream was almost cold.

Well, that was about all that happened right then, except for one other thing. And it was that one thing that helped make our next adventure, a fishing trip for walleyes, extraordinarily interesting and exciting.

Not having brought along any extra clothes, I had to walk in my wet pants back to our station wagon, which wasn't any too much fun for me. There they made me lie down where I wouldn't be seen while some of the gang wrung the water out of my trousers and also out of the tail of my shirt. I would have to wait till they dried enough for me to put them on, and that meant I had to let the rest of the gang visit a very special curio shop without me, while my clothes were hanging on a limb in the sun.

Poetry, who was about my best friend, was already sorry I was all wet, and we made up as soon as I found out he was going to stay with me to keep me company.

I gave Little Jim some money out of my bill-fold and told him to pick out something he especially thought my little sister, Charlotte Ann, would like. I knew that in a few days we were all going to break camp and drive back to Sugar Creek, and I wanted to take home a few things made by the Indians.

Poetry and I were alone awhile, with me lying under a blanket on the backseat of the station wagon. We talked over all the wonderful experiences of our vacation and decided it had been the best camping trip we'd had in our lives.

"Only one thing would make it the best we ever *could* have," he said, and when I said, "What?" he didn't answer for a minute.

He was sitting in the open car door not far from me, and I was lying on my back, wishing the hot sun and the breeze would hurry up and get my clothes a little drier so I could put them on. He had his back to me, so I couldn't see his face, but his squawky voice had a sort of a far-away sound in it as though he was thinking of something very serious.

When he still didn't answer me, I asked him again, and he said quietly, "I feel sorry for

Tom." Then his voice sort of choked, and I guessed that he liked that little red-haired guy just as well as I did.

Right that second, if anybody had asked me anything, I couldn't have answered either. I felt my eyes stinging, and there would have been a tear in my voice, and boys don't like to have anybody see tears in their eyes or hear them in their voices.

Pretty soon, though, Poetry spoke again with his back still toward me, "Did you ever read this verse in the Bible?"

If I hadn't been already down, you could have knocked me over with a fish scale when I realized what he was doing. He had taken his little leather New Testament out of his shirt pocket and, looking through it, had found a verse he thought was extra good.

As you maybe know, an official part of the equipment of anybody who belongs to the Sugar Creek Gang is a small New Testament. We each carry one nearly all the time, and every one of us not only reads it every day, but we aren't ashamed to let anybody know we do, either.

But on account of being boys and feeling the way nearly all boys do, we didn't talk about the Bible very much, except in campfire meetings or at Sunday school, and only once in a while when two or three of us were together.

Little Jim and I did more of that than any of the rest of us. That's because he—well, he had a keen mind and thought more about the

Bible, I guess, and was always getting such good ideas. Also Little Jim was just glad he was alive. Not a boy in the world *would* be alive if God hadn't made him and also if God didn't *keep* him alive. And there isn't a boy in the world that's dumb enough to want to be dead, which is why a boy ought to be glad to love God and to be kind to Him. Little Jim always was.

Anyway, when Poetry asked me if I had ever read "this verse," I said, "What verse?"

So he read it to me, with his back still turned. It was out of the book of Matthew, chapter 18, and was the nineteenth verse. It said, "If two of you agree on earth about anything that they may ask, it shall be done for them by My Father who is in heaven."

It made me feel good inside to even think about the Bible, especially since I knew both of us believed what we were talking about. I just lay there, looking through the station wagon window up at the pretty branches of a pine tree that grew not far away. I was also listening to the gurgling of the water close by and felt something sort of warm in my heart, as though Poetry and God and I had a secret of some kind.

When we finished telling each other what we thought the verse meant, we made up our minds that we were going to stick together and pray until Little Tom's dad was saved.

"Let's shake on it," Poetry said. He swung around and shoved his hand in my direction.

I grabbed it quick and said, "Shake."

"Shake," he said again, then we prayed together for Tom's dad, and I felt good inside.

I noticed the branches of the pine tree above me were swaying in the wind, and I knew my clothes were drying pretty fast—I hoped.

A little later we heard the gang coming. I knew it was the gang because it sounded like a flock of blackbirds gathering in the woods in a Sugar Creek autumn, getting ready for migrating to a warmer country. It also sounded like a flock of crows with a few scolding blue jays mixed in with them and maybe a harsh-voiced shrieking kingfisher joining in. Dragonfly was the rattling-voiced kingfisher and Circus the scolding blue jay.

My clothes were dry enough for me to put on if, while we drove along, I'd sit on the leather seat of the station wagon, which I did. Away we went, back to camp and to the next day's fishing trip.

"Look what I got for Charlotte Ann," Little Jim said and shoved over to me a couple of small balloons. "They cost only ten cents apiece," he said proudly and handed me my change.

I was a little disappointed but didn't want to say so, because Little Jim had such a happy grin on his face to think he had saved me money. And I was also sure Charlotte Ann would be happy to see the balloons blown up nice and big. Most babies laugh and reach out their hands for them the very minute they see them.

I tucked the two balloons in my shirt pocket beside my New Testament and buttoned the flap and forgot about them.

The next day was our very special fishing trip for walleyed pike. Boy oh boy, it was going to be a wonderful trip, I thought. We were going to fish, not for small fish such as bluegills and crappies, which people call "pan" fish, but for big walleyes to pack and ship home to our folks at Sugar Creek. Also, we were going to keep our eyes open every second to see if we could find any trace of John Till.

6

I was certainly glad our little Indian friend Snow-in-the-Face was well enough to be our guide on our fishing trip for walleye. As you maybe know, he'd been very sick. But almost right away after our gang had gone to see him, he had started to get better. And now, today, he was coming to our camp to visit us and to guide us to the best fishing waters for walleyed pike, so that we could all catch our "limit," which is eight walleyes apiece. Multiplying eight fish by seven boys, which any teacher will tell you you can't do, we'd have fifty-six fish to pack in ice and ship back to Sugar Creek for our parents to see and to help us eat. Boy oh boy, it was going to be fun!

About three o'clock that afternoon, after the gang had all had a rest hour, Snow-in-the-Face and his big brother, Eagle Eye, came gliding in a canoe straight to our shore.

There was a lot of excitement around camp for a while as all of us finished getting our equipment ready. And we made sure our two big fishing boats were equipped with life preservers, which nobody ought to go on a fishing trip without.

It had been a terribly hot day, and the sun poured its yellowish heat down on us something fierce as our boats plowed their wet way out across the waves toward an island. It also reflected back up into our faces from the water and made me glad I had on a pair of dark glasses to protect my eyes from the extrabright light.

Snow-in-the-Face was in the boat I was in, along with Little Jim, Poetry, and Dragonfly. We were following the other boat, which had Eagle Eye and Big Jim and Circus and Little Tom Till. Barry had stayed home to write letters and to look after camp.

In a little while our boats neared the pretty pine- and spruce-covered island and circled around to the other side, where we anchored in a little cove, not more than thirty yards from each other in some quiet water.

That super little reddish-brown-faced Indian with his bright black eyes and straight black hair didn't even use a fishing pole. Instead, he had a big heavy line, which he dropped down over the side of our boat.

I was sitting beside him in the middle seat. Poetry was in the stern, close to the outboard motor. Dragonfly was in the prow. Little Jim was in front of me in a seat by himself, with his life vest on, which meant he was even safer than the rest of us. If our boat upset or we fell out, he would be ready to float to shore without having to hold onto a pillow.

In a minute we all had our hooks baited with live chubs and were waiting for somebody—either in our boat or in the other one—to catch the first fish. The very second one of us would get a walleye, we'd know we'd found a school of them, and in a little while we'd all get bites and catch fish at the same time, because walleyes stick together like a gang of boys.

"Eagle Eye found this place last year," Snow-in-the-Face said. "Fish bite here when they don't anyplace else on the lake."

But after we all had sat there and waited and waited and pulled our lines in and out of the water for an hour and not a one of us had caught a single fish or even had a nibble, it looked as if having a good guide wasn't working.

Snow-in-the-Face had a pucker on his brown forehead and looked worried.

Ho hum, I thought and shifted myself to another uncomfortable position on the hot boat seat. Any position is uncomfortable when the fish don't bite and the deerflies are swarming around your legs and hands and biting fiercely just the way you wish the fish would.

Pretty soon I looked over at the pretty pine-covered island and wished I could go over there and sit in the shade for a while. I was also remembering that was the very island I'd wanted to explore when I'd first gotten the idea of playing *Robinson Crusoe* and *Treasure Island.* That was the idea that had got us tangled up in the mystery of the buried treasure, most of which we'd finally found. The rest of it old John Till probably had somewhere, wherever he was, which nobody knew.

"I'm terribly hot," I said to the rest of us in our boat. "Let's go over to that island and lie down in the shade a while." The others thought it was a good idea, so we took in our lazy lines and pulled up anchor and rowed over.

In a little while, Poetry and I were strolling along, following the shore around to the side where we could see our camp away out across the lake. It was one of the prettiest islands I'd seen. It had big Norway pines and spruce and tamarack and ferns and all kinds of wildflowers, such as red columbine and white goldthread. In a boggy place were some pitcher plants, which had weird-looking green leaves that looked like one of the green pitchers Mom has on our sideboard at home. The leaves looked like the lips of a French horn that one of the men at Sugar Creek plays in the band on Saturday night.

We'd left Snow-in-the-Face and Little Jim and Dragonfly back at the shore with the boat, because Snow-in-the-Face and Little Jim had acted as though they didn't want to come with us, and Dragonfly had been lazy and also was afraid of smelling wildflowers and having to sneeze a lot. That was one of the reasons he'd come on this vacation with us—so he could get away from Sugar Creek flowers and timothy hay and ragweed and everything else that would make him sneeze.

"You know what?" Poetry said to me all of a sudden, and when I said, "No, what?" he said, "This would be a good island for John Till to hide on. Maybe when he got out of the ice-house, he came over here."

"But how could he get here? We had his boat."

"He might swim," Poetry said.

But that wasn't a good idea, because it was pretty far from any other shore to here, so I said, "Of course, he could rent a boat from almost any resort up here."

We were standing close to a sandy beach, and the waves were washing up in a very lazy friendly way, when all of a sudden Poetry said, "Look, somebody's been here not long ago. Somebody's had a boat beached here on the sand."

Somebody had, but it was gone now.

"Boy oh boy!" I said, all of a sudden getting excited. "And here are shoe tracks, going back into the island somewhere."

We decided to follow the tracks, but we didn't find anything interesting. There might have been a broken twig trail, though, like the one we'd followed before, and which you know about, but we couldn't find a thing, so we gave up and went back to Dragonfly and Snow-in-the-Face and Little Jim.

"Where were you guys?" Dragonfly wanted to know, and I said, "Oh, looking for buried treasure."

Snow-in-the-Face got a strange, faraway expression on his face, squinted his eyes, and said, "Sometimes we see lights out here at night."

And then it was Dragonfly's turn to get a strange, faraway expression, as if he wished he was as far away as his thoughts.

Well, we decided to try fishing some more, like the rest of the guys in the other boat, though they still hadn't caught anything either. We rowed out to another place and baited our hooks and tried again.

Another hour passed, during which we pulled anchor and tried a half-dozen different locations, and still not a one of us caught a single fish. We were terribly discouraged.

"You can have one if you *want* one," Little Jim said.

"How?" I said.

And he said, "One of those balloons I bought for you yesterday is a rubber fish. You can blow it up—maybe it's a walleye."

Well, I still had those two balloons in my shirt pocket, so because I was terribly bored and didn't know what else to do, I pulled out the one that looked as if it would be fish-shaped when it was blown up. And like the wolf that ate up the little pigs, I huffed and I puffed and I blew the balloon up into a nice big fish that looked like a walleyed pike. For a while I had something to keep my mind off being bored, because if there is anything that is harder to do than anything else, it is to sit on the seat of a boat on a hot day when the fish won't bite.

"If we get *one,* we'll get twenty," Poetry said. "Walleyes go in schools, you know."

"Yeah," Little Jim piped up, "but fish maybe don't *have* school in August," which reminded me that right after August came September, and generally in the first week of September the Sugar Creek School started and . . .

I let out a fierce long sigh when I thought of that, not because I didn't need an education, but I hated to have to sit down to get one, which is what you have to do in school most of the time. The boat seat was getting harder and harder every minute.

The yellow rubber fish I'd just blown up looked cute, though, and was as fat as a butterball. For a while I let it float on the water out to the end of the fishing line I had tied it on.

"Here, Poetry," I said to the fish, "get out there and float. You're so fat you *can't* sink."

That made the real Poetry pretend to be mad, and he said to me, "Oh, you go jump in the lake!"

And then, all of a sudden, Poetry got a big strike! He waited until he was sure it was time to set the hook, which he did at exactly the right time, and he landed a very excited walleye. Only it wasn't much bigger than a big yellow perch—hardly big enough to keep.

"OK, Bill, hand me the stringer," he ordered me, panting with happiness. Talk about a proud grin on a boy's face! Poetry really had one.

"What stringer?" I said and looked all around on the bottom of the boat for one. And—would you believe this?—not a one of us had brought along a fish stringer! The other boat was too far away for them to throw one into our boat, so Poetry just sat there with his fish in his hand, wondering what to do with it.

"It's too little to keep," Little Jim said. "Let him go back to his mama."

"I wish I knew where his mama is hiding," Dragonfly said. "I'd like to catch *her*."

"Let him go, and he'll *find* his mama," Snow-in-the-Face said, and he had the cutest grin on his small face. I could see he was as mischievous as any other boy.

"It's probably a little lost child fish," Little Jim said. "We aren't going to catch any more anyway. Let's let him go home to his parents."

Well, I had the end of my fish balloon tied airtight shut with a piece of old fishing line I'd had in my pocket, and it was still in the water on the opposite side of the boat. It was really cute, that little yellowish rubber fish, bobbing along out there on the surface.

And then Poetry yelled across to the other boat, saying, "Hey, you guys over there! We got a fish but don't have any stringer to put him on. What'll we do with him?"

Circus, being mischievous and having lots of bright ideas anyway, yelled back to us, "If you'll put him back in the water and tell him to swim over here, we'll put him on *our* stringer."

And that was what gave Poetry another idea, which wasn't so dumb and which turned our discouraged fishing trip into a one that was wonderful. Poetry yelled to Circus, "Super idea! We'll send him over right away!" Then he got a command in his voice and said to me, "Here,

Bill, give me that line." He reached out and took it before I could make up my mind not to let him have it.

"What crazy thing are you going to do?" Dragonfly asked.

Poetry held his fish between his knees a minute while he made a double slipknot around the walleye's tail. And then almost before anybody could have stopped him if he had wanted to, Poetry released that frisky little walleye into the water sort of the way my mother does when she carefully holds an old setting hen and eases her into a coop where there is a nestful of eggs to sit on. Poetry said to the fish, as he let go, "Here, Wally, my friend, you go swimming straight for the other boat away over there!"

That fish certainly had lots of pep. Being out of the water for that short time hadn't hurt him a bit—although, if you are going to let a fish go free after catching him, you are supposed to be very careful to handle him with wet hands and release him under the water rather than throw him back, and he'll be more likely to live.

The frisky walleye made a fierce fast dive straight down into the water, and in a few seconds the yellow balloon was bobbing up and down as if it was a boy's bobber on a fishing line. And it started to move right in the direction of the other boat—kind of slow, but actually toward it!

Poetry sighed proudly, leaned back, stuck

his thumbs in his armpits, and said, "See there, fish understand my language."

That made Dragonfly say, "That's because you talk like a fish," which, for Dragonfly, was almost a bright remark.

I could see, though, that the balloon fish was changing its course, which meant that the real fish was too. It began working its way a little toward the left, out toward deeper water and farther from shore. We all watched it, having fun, and Poetry kept yelling to it to turn to the right and to hurry up. But pretty soon, when it was maybe fifty yards from us, it stopped going in one direction and began to move slowly around in a small circle.

"I'll bet he's caught on a snag," Snow-in-the-Face said, and it seemed that he might be right, because, even though the balloon bobbed around a little, it didn't move any farther away but just seemed to stay more or less in the same place.

Well, we fished on, all of us hoping for another fish, but not a one of us caught one, so pretty soon we got discouraged again and pulled up anchor.

Then Poetry said, "Why don't we go get him, then go home and everybody go swimming?"

It sounded like a good idea. It'd be a lot more fun to do that than to sit on a hard boat seat watching a rubber balloon bobbing on the surface of a lake that didn't have any hungry fish in it.

"Let's troll over," Snow-in-the-Face said.

"Sometimes when you can't catch fish any other way, they'll bite when you do that."

Dragonfly said it was a good idea, too, because there might be a "lost, strayed, or stolen" fish all by itself between here and the balloon.

So we all left our lines in the water while Snow-in-the-Face and Little Jim took the oars and rowed us splashily out toward that nice yellow balloon I was going to get and take home to Charlotte Ann.

We were almost there, and I was getting ready to reach out my hand and get the balloon, when quick as a flash I saw Little Jim's line go taut! His pole bent down clear to the water, while he dropped his oar and quick grabbed his pole and yelled excitedly, "Hey, I've got a fish!"

Just then Dragonfly's line did the same thing, and then—*wham!*—my own line went tight. And the next thing we knew, most of us in our boat found ourselves in the middle of one of the most exciting fishing experiences of our whole lives. We yelled and pulled, and our lines went singing out as our reels unwound. And almost at the same time, Dragonfly and Little Jim and Poetry and I all landed a walleye apiece and laid them, flopping and splashing water in every direction, in the bottom of the boat.

"We've struck a school!" Poetry cried. "My fish took us right to them! He knew exactly where they were!"

7

Well, you aren't supposed to yell like a lot of wild men on the warpath when you start catching a lot of fish, because you might scare the fish away. So almost right away we all shushed each other and only made some noise when we caught a fish, which was just about as fast as we could bait our hooks and get our lines into the water again.

We quick anchored right close to where the balloon was, and the other boat carrying the rest of the gang came rowing over as quietly as they could and anchored close by.

Talk about excitement! We'd never had so much fishing fun in our whole lives as we were having right that minute. And then, just like Sugar Creek School getting out and the kids tumbling out the door and all going away from the red brick schoolhouse, our school of wall-eyes moved on, and we stopped getting bites.

I knew *something* was going to happen the minute I saw the yellow balloon start moving fast out toward deeper water.

"Look!" Dragonfly, who saw it first, said. "Wally acts like he's scared. Look at him go!"

Everybody looked. The balloon was bobbing up and down and even diving all the way under. Then it stayed under for a long time before bouncing back up and shooting almost a foot into the air and landing *ker-smack* on the water again.

But we had enough fish for one day, so Big Jim said, "Let's go back to camp and get supper," which was a good idea. We would come back tomorrow.

"What'll we do with Wally?" Poetry asked.

"He's been a good friend," Dragonfly said. "He ought to have some kind of appreciation."

Then Little Jim piped up good and loud, saying, "Let's give him his liberty!"

Well, we had enough larger fish, and Wally really deserved some kind of a reward for helping us catch so many fish to take home to Sugar Creek. So we pulled anchor and rowed out toward where Wally was making the balloon fish bob around in such a lively style.

As soon as the boat had eased alongside, I reached down my hand, caught hold of the balloon, and started to haul Wally in toward the boat. But then my line went tight as though it was fastened onto a snag down on the bottom of the lake.

I gave a tug but not too hard, because I didn't want the line to scale off any scales from Wally's tail. It is as hard on a fish to lose some of its scales as on a barefoot boy to stub his toe and knock the skin off.

"He's tangled up on something," I said and gave another small pull. And then—*wham!* There was a fierce wild lunge down there somewhere, and I felt a scared feeling race up and down my spine. I knew Wally didn't have *that* much strength. Whatever it was felt as big as an excited pig running in our barnyard back at Sugar Creek.

I had hold of the line as well as the balloon, and the line was cutting into my hands. I couldn't think straight but knew I didn't dare let loose.

Snow-in-the-Face, for the very first time, got excited and yelled something to Eagle Eye in their Indian language and then to us in English, "Some great big fish has swallowed him!"

I held on, in spite of the line's hurting my hand a little, and then, out there about ten feet, something with a big, long, ugly snout and fierce eyes shot up through the waves and almost two feet in the air, then dive-splashed back in again.

There was a ferocious boiling of the surface as if a bomb had exploded down in the water somewhere. I was trembling inside the way any fisherman trembles when a fierce fast-fighting fish gets away after it's been hooked—only this one hadn't been hooked with a real hook.

He had probably come swimming along down there, looking for an early supper, like a robin hopping around on our lawn at Sugar Creek looking for night crawlers, and, seeing Wally swimming lazily around, he had decided to eat him.

He had probably slowly nosed his ugly long snout up to Wally and then all of a sudden made a savage rush at him with his mouth open, had swallowed him whole, and started to swim away. That had scared all the other fish, which was why we'd all stopped getting bites at the same time.

Anyway, right after that fighting fish lunged up out of the water and down in again, he made a dive straight for our boat, shot under it, and pulled so hard that I had to hold on for dear life. If I'd had a long line on a fishing rod with a reel, I could have let the reel spin, as fishermen do when they have a wild walleye or an enormous northern pike on their lines. I could have "played" him until he was tired out, then hauled him in. But with my line only a dozen or more feet long, I was pretty sure I didn't have a chance in the world to land him, and the next thing I knew, I found out I was right.

Seconds, it seemed, after he dived under our boat, I felt my line go sickeningly slack, and I knew I'd lost him. I couldn't tell whether he'd broken my line or whether he'd swallowed backwards and Wally was free again.

The gang was groaning with disappointment, because everybody had seen what had happened. And while I was pulling in the lifeless line to see what was on the other end, I had a sick feeling in the pit of my stomach, the kind a fisherman gets when he loses a big fish.

And then I was holding up the end of the line for us to look at.

Dragonfly, seeing it, said, "Poetry's slipknot slipped."

We would have been a terribly sad gang if

we hadn't already caught a lot of middle-sized walleyes.

Circus called to us from the other boat and said, "We could have put a lot of kidnapper's ransom money in a fish that big, if we'd caught him."

"There wouldn't have been much room left with Wally already inside of him," Poetry said.

For some reason I was looking at Little Jim when Poetry said that, and I noticed a sad expression come over his small, mouselike face. I thought he had a couple of tears in his eyes.

But it had been a wonderful fishing trip, and we couldn't afford to cry over a lost northern pike, which is what we all decided the big fish was. So after the other boat had pulled anchor, we started our motors and steered around the island toward camp with our caught fish lying in the bottom of the boat.

Little Jim was sitting in the seat in front of me, facing me as we roared along with Poetry running the motor. Different ones of us were talking and yelling to each other about all the different things that had happened—all except Little Jim, who, I noticed, was extra quiet, and his eyes still had that sad look in them.

Pretty soon I leaned over and half whispered to him, "What's the matter?"

He swallowed, then said, "Nothing."

"There is, too," I said, just as he turned his head and gave it a quick shake. When he looked back in my direction, the tears that'd been in his eyes a second before were gone.

That is the way Little Jim gets tears out of his eyes—he just turns his head away, jerks it real quick, and that shakes the tears out.

Dragonfly, who knew Little Jim had that cute way of getting tears out without using a handkerchief, so that nobody would know he had had tears in the first place, saw him do that and said to him from behind me, "Don't you know tears are salty? Freshwater fish that live in lakes don't *like* salt water."

"That's *not* funny," I said to Dragonfly over my shoulder, mad at him for not having more respect for Little Jim's hurt heart. I knew Little Jim's heart was hurt when he said to me, "That wasn't much of a reward for Wally, after all he did for us."

Then just as sometimes happens to my mother when she says something that has a sad thought mixed up with it, Little Jim's eyes got a couple of *new* tears in them, which he quick shook out into the lake. Then he said, as he reached his small hands toward me, "Let me hold the balloon fish for a while."

I pushed the yellow balloon toward him, and the way he took it, made me think of the way my little two-year-old baby sister, Charlotte Ann, would reach out her chubby little hands for it when I got home and showed it to her.

For a minute, while our two boats plowed along through the water—which, with the sunlight shining on the moving waves, looked like a big lakeful of live silver—my thoughts took a hop, skip, and jump across the lake to the shore. I leaped over the Chippewa Forest and high up over a lot of other lakes, like Paul Bunyan himself.

And all of a sudden I landed right inside our kitchen at Sugar Creek, where I knew I'd be in just a few days. In my mind's eye, I saw Mom standing by our kitchen stove near the east window, which has a green ivy vine trailing across the top of the outside of it. I could smell the aroma of raw-fried potatoes frying and see the steam puffing up from the hooked spout of our old teakettle.

If, when I came in, I accidently carried in a little mud on my shoes or bare feet, Mom would say, as she nearly always does, "Would you like to get the broom, Bill, and sweep out that mud which a little while ago came walking in on two feet?"

I would know whose two feet she meant, and I'd grin, and right away I'd step to the place where we keep our broom, which is behind the kitchen door. I wouldn't any more than get started with the dustpan and broom than Mom would say, "Be careful not to sweep *hard,* or we'll have dust in our fried potatoes."

While I was doing that, all of a sudden I'd get tangled up with something, and, turning around, I'd see my neat little sister, Charlotte Ann, with her tiny toy broom, sweeping it around awkwardly the way little girls do when they're just learning how to sweep.

Now that she's learned to walk, she tries to do everything any of the rest of us do. She follows Mom around, sweeping when Mom does, washing her hands when Mom does, and when Mom or Dad sit down to read a book or a magazine, *she* gets a book or a magazine and tries to read, nearly always getting it upside down, though. Sometimes when Mom is getting supper and Charlotte Ann can't see high enough to see what Mom is doing, she gets cross and whines and fusses and pulls at Mom's dress or apron and makes a nuisance out of herself. She doesn't know she's a nuisance. Maybe she thinks Mom is making a nuisance of *herself,* instead, for not letting her help get supper.

Yes sir, I was getting homesick for my folks and could hardly wait till I got home next week to tell them all the exciting adventures we'd had. Also, it'd be fun to watch the mail every day to see if maybe Little Jim would get any letters from anybody who would find the gospel messages that he'd been tossing out into the lake in whiskey bottles.

Thinking that, I remembered John Till and wondered where he was and what he was doing.

And all of a sudden I remembered what Poetry and I had been thinking and talking about in the station wagon when we'd been at the source of the Mississippi River. He had found a Bible verse that said if any two of the Lord's disciples were agreed about something they wanted to pray for, they could pray for it, and the heavenly Father would do it.

Thinking that, I turned around to Poetry, who was running the boat, and looked at him, and he looked at me. I pointed to my shirt pocket, which had its flap buttoned to keep my New Testament from falling out.

His eyes looked where my finger was pointing, and the expression on his mischievous happy-looking face changed to a very sober one. He squinted his eyes as a boy does when he's thinking about something or somebody someplace else. He lifted his free hand (the other being on the rubber grip of the motor's handle) and, with his forefinger, pointed to his own shirt pocket. We just looked into each other's eyes a minute, and for some reason I felt fine inside.

Then I swung my eyes around over the lake and in the direction where the sun was going to set after a while. I was glad I was alive—for the same reason Little Jim was glad he was alive. In a little while, we'd be to shore.

There was only one thing about a fishing trip I didn't like, and that was having to help clean the fish afterward. But, boy oh boy, when you start sinking your teeth into the nice snow-white fish steaks, which restaurants' menus call *fillet,* you don't mind having had to clean them at all. *Yum, yum, crunch, crunch* . . . Boy oh boy, I certainly was hungry.

As our boat cut a wide circle and swung up beside the dock in front of our big brown tents, I could see that a fire was already started in the Indian kitchen we'd made. That meant that, just the minute we had our fish cleaned, Barry'd have them sizzling in the skillet for us.

That night just before we went to bed, Tom and I were alone a minute at the end of the dock, and he had both hands clasped around the slender flagpole. He was swaying his body forward and backward and sideways, not saying anything for a while, and neither was I. Then he said, "I wish I could find my dad."

There was a tear in his voice, and I knew he was feeling pretty awful inside, and because I liked him, I felt the same way for a minute.

"Nobody knows where he is," I said.

And Tom surprised me by saying, "Only *one* Person knows."

As quick as I realized what he meant, I said, "Yes, that's right. He knows everything in the world at the same time."

The moon shining on the water looked the way it nearly always does in the moonlight— like silver or like a field of oats on Dad's farm would look if somebody had painted it white and the wind was blowing.

Santa, who had his cabin not far up the lake from where we were camped, had gone away for the night, and Big Jim and Circus had been selected to stay all night in his cabin to sort of look after things for him. They were the biggest members of our gang, and Barry gave them permission.

All the rest of the gang were in the tents, maybe undressing, and Tom and I were really alone, when all of a sudden I heard a sound on the shore and a voice calling in a low husky whisper, "Tom! Hey—Tom!" And I was sure I had heard the voice before.

Then I saw the bushes part and a dark form move out into the moonlight. At the same time Tom let go of the flagpole and made a dive for the shore, beating it up the dock as fast as he could.

I was so surprised I couldn't move. I felt weak in the knees and sick at the stomach. Tom was over there in a flash, and I watched him and somebody standing side by side, talking in whispers.

Then the dark form I'd seen come out of the bushes darted back again, and a second later I heard footsteps going *lickety-sizzle* up the lakeshore.

Then Tom started back to me, and I met him in the middle of the dock.

"Who was it?" I asked, thinking I knew. "Was it your dad?"

"No," Tom said, "it was my brother, Bob. I gave him the letter from Mother, and he's going to give it to Dad."

8

Can you imagine that? Big Bob Till, Big Jim's worst enemy and, except for Big Jim, the fiercest fighter in the whole country anywhere, maybe! He was what people called a "juvenile delinquent," which means he didn't like to behave himself and had done many things that were against the law.

Maybe I'd better tell you right now, in case you don't know it, that Mr. Foote, Little Jim's dad, had used his influence back at Sugar Creek to keep Bob from having to go to reform school. Then Bob had been paroled to him. Little Jim had been glad, because he'd rather anybody would be *good* than to have him be *bad* and have to be punished for it.

But Bob was still not behaving himself, because he hadn't been trained at home like most of the rest of us. Even we were having a hard enough time to be even half as good as we thought we were, and we had had training all our boy lives.

When Tom said to me, there in the moonlight on the middle of the dock, that he'd given his mom's letter to his brother, and I realized that Bob was up here in the north woods, you could have knocked me over with a moonbeam, I was so surprised. Of course, he was gone now—somewhere or other—but where?

I asked Tom a question then. "Where *is* your dad?"

And he said, "I don't know, but Bob does, and he'll take Mother's letter to him."

It seemed the rest of the gang ought to know Bob was up here, and for some reason it seemed that Poetry ought to know it first. So the very second I had a chance after I got into our tent a little later, and the lights were out, and Dragonfly had been quieted down from talking and laughing—in fact, his noisy nose sounded as if he was asleep—I reached out my hand and touched Poetry and said, "You asleep?"

And he whispered quietly, "Yes," which meant he wasn't. So I told him about Bob, and he said, "That explains a lot of things."

"What, for instance?" I asked.

And he said, "It explains who opened the icehouse door and let John Till out."

Then Poetry and I decided to get up and go outside where we could talk without being heard.

I was surprised we were able to get up and out without being stopped by Dragonfly's waking up and asking questions or insisting on going along. He is never able to let a guy have any secrets without wanting them to be divided up with him.

A good place to talk without being heard would be down at the dock, we decided, so away we went toward the lake, where the waves were sighing and lapping against the shore and dock posts and making the boats rock a little. One boat was making a little scraping noise against the dock.

"Where was Bob standing?" Poetry asked, and when I pointed to the bushes, he started straight toward them. As you maybe know, he wanted to be a detective someday and was always looking for what detectives and the police and the FBI call "clues." And often Poetry was finding one—or something he thought was one.

As soon as we were both behind the bushes, where nobody at camp could see us, he turned on his flashlight and shined it all around where Bob and Tom had been standing.

"What're we looking for?" I asked.

He answered as he always does, "A clue."

"What kind of a clue?" I asked.

And he replied, "I'll tell you just as soon as I find it."

Well, I certainly didn't expect we'd find anything, but all of a sudden I heard a sound from up the shore like footsteps coming, so I said in a husky whisper, "I think I *heard* a clue coming from somewhere." Then, up the path and not far away I saw a flashlight blink on and off.

We crouched low, hardly daring to breathe, knowing that somebody was coming for sure and wondering who it was and what he wanted. Was it Bob Till or maybe old hook-nosed John Till himself?

Right that second, though, I saw something white lying where my feet had been a moment before. It looked like a folded white handkerchief, so I stooped down, reached out my hand to touch it, and it was an envelope.

Little Tom's mom's letter, I thought. *Bob dropped it and is coming back to look for it.*

Poetry and I kept even quieter than we had been. He did not know, of course, what I'd just found and tucked into my pajama pocket. We had not taken time to dress—I was in my green-and-white striped pajamas and Poetry in his purple ones.

We both had the weird feeling that for some reason we should get ourselves out of there, which we did. We sneaked back maybe fifteen feet before deciding to stop and wait to see who it was and what he was looking for and why, if we could.

In a few excited moments, whoever was coming was right where we ourselves had been and was flashing his flashlight on and off all around where a little while before I'd picked up the envelope. I could see he wasn't very tall—not as tall as big John Till—so I decided it might be Bob again.

Poetry had hold of my arm so tight it actually hurt, which showed, even though he was usually calm in a time of excitement, that this time he was pretty tense himself.

I certainly didn't know what to do and would have been afraid to do it even if I had. But I wouldn't have had time to do much of anything. Right that second, whoever it was stopped searching, and I heard his footsteps going on past in the direction of Santa's dock, which was several hundred yards farther on.

I thought of the envelope in my pocket and remembered that it wasn't mine and that I ought to call out to whoever it was and say, "Hey, there, mister, whatever you're looking for, I've got it. Whatever it is!" But I didn't.

Then Poetry and I were alone with ourselves, and the only sound was the friendly lapping of the waves against the dock posts and the washing of other waves against the sandy shore. Away out on the lake was a great big shimmering silver spot of moonlight, which was very pretty. Still farther was the shadow of the trees on the little island on the other side of which we had caught our walleyes and where Wally had lost his life. Right that minute he was maybe half digested in the stomach of a big ugly-snouted northern pike.

I could feel my heart beating with excitement, but there was something else I was feeling too. It was the envelope I had in my pocket, which I quick took out.

I whispered for Poetry to turn on his light, which he did, and this is what we saw on the envelope, written in pencil that was kind of smeared the way pencil marks on a letter are when a boy has carried it around in his pocket or in his hands awhile. We saw written in a big awkward scrawl the name Bob Till. But there wasn't anything else, not even an address—and no postage stamp.

Quick as anything, not stopping to think that that letter was private property and he had no right to open it, Poetry had a paper out of the envelope and was unfolding it, and I was holding his trembling flashlight on it to see what it said. It was a sheet of white typewriter paper, and there wasn't a thing on it, not even a pencil mark.

"It's another invisible-ink map," Poetry said, and I remembered the other one we'd found. I told you about it in another story. When we'd warmed it up, it had turned out to be a map, showing where the little kidnapped girl had been found and which way two broken twig trails led. And we had followed them and finally found the ransom money in the old ice-house.

"And here's a *note*," Poetry whispered, as a little folded piece of paper with writing on it tumbled out.

That note, which was also printed in pencil, said,

Dear Bob:
Santa's away tonight. Get my boat which is tied to his dock and pick me up at the Indian cemetery at 10 o'clock and we'll get the rest of the ransom money. If I'm not there, wait till I come.

Your Dad

Well, when I saw what Poetry's trembling flashlight showed us was written on that unfolded piece of paper, you could have knocked me over with a question mark. Our mystery had come to life again, and we were going to have another exciting adventure before our vacation was over. Hurrah! Boy oh boy!

Poetry spoke first, saying excitedly, "I'll bet Bob's going down to get the boat right now! We've got to stop him!"

"Why?" I said.

And he said, "Stop him and make him tell us where his dad is. Then we or the police can capture him."

"Bob wouldn't tell us," I said, being sure he wouldn't.

"Well, for pity's sake, we must do *something!*" Poetry exclaimed.

When I said, "What?" he said, "Get the gang and beat Bob to the cemetery!"

That made as good sense as anything I could have thought of, especially since right that minute I heard a motorboat somewhere and guessed that Bob had already started the powerful black-shrouded motor that was on the boat John Till had had and which the police had left at Santa's dock.

We didn't have time to decide anything right then, though. Almost as quick as a lightning bug can flash its light on and off, we heard somebody running toward us from the direction of Santa's cottage. A second later, *two* forms came puffing out into the moonlight and into our camp. It was Big Jim and Circus, who should have been staying all night in Santa's cabin just to sort of look after things for him.

I thought of Tom Till and hated to have *him* know what was going on, which he would if there was a lot of boy noise and the whole camp should wake up and come scrambling over each other down to the dock in crazy-looking pajamas, talking and wondering, *What on earth?*

So Poetry and I shushed Big Jim and Circus, and the four of us started to tell each other what we knew.

"Somebody took John Till's boat!" Circus puffed. "Hear him? There he goes now!"

About two hundred yards from shore, I saw the shadow of a boat in the moonlight, heard the roar of a powerful motor, and knew we'd have to hurry to get to the Indian cemetery first.

"Let's step on the gas and get going," Circus said as soon as we'd told them about the note we had found.

Poetry asked, "What kind of gas—outboard motor or station wagon?"

Big Jim, knowing that most of the Sugar Creek Gang had more bravery than good sense and that we sometimes did dangerous things without thinking first, said, "This is another job for the police."

But Poetry spoke up and said, "Let's be policemen ourselves! By the time we phone them and they could get there, it'd be too late."

Which it would be, I thought. So we decided we ought to try to get to the cemetery first by driving there as fast as we could in the station wagon.

What to do about Tom was our first problem, and we wouldn't have much time to try to solve it. Some of us simply had to get going to the cemetery to be there before Bob could get to The Narrows and zip through them into the lake where the cemetery was.

It was half past nine right that second, and Bob was supposed to meet his dad there at ten. If only we could get there before either one of them did—and hide somewhere in the bushes. Then maybe we could sneak up on them and get both of them at once—because it looked as if Bob was in on the business of being a helper to the kidnapper too.

Barry and Little Jim and Tom were the only ones left in Barry's tent. Barry must have heard our excited talk, because his tent flap plopped open and out he came, wanting to know what on earth all the excitement was about. We told him and showed him the note, and then he also heard Bob's motor on the lake. We didn't stop to try to figure out why John Till had *written* to Bob instead of just telling him where to meet him.

And then Little Jim and Tom came tumbling out of Barry's tent in our direction, and Dragonfly came out of the other tent, and there we all were—too many and some of us too little to go on a kidnapper hunt.

Barry took charge of things quick. He said, "You boys all stay right here and look after camp. I've a phone call to make—and I want to see the fire warden a minute."

And I guess I never was so disappointed in my life as I was right that minute.

"Is there a fire somewhere?" Tom Till asked quick, sniffing to see if anything smelled like smoke.

Dragonfly did the same thing and sneezed just as if he had actually smelled something he was allergic to.

A bit later, Barry in the station wagon was driving down the lane toward Santa's boathouse, and I knew that in a few seconds he'd be pulling up a steep hill, following the sandy trail at the top, and going like mad down a winding road through the forest to the fire warden's house, which you know about if you've read *Screams in the Night.*

There he'd make a terribly fast phone call to the police—or else let the fire warden's wife do it while he and the fire warden beat it on to the Indian cemetery. They'd probably stop before they got there, though, and sneak carefully up along the lakeshore to where Bob's boat would be coming in. Then, if they could, they'd capture both Bob and his dad.

I felt terribly disappointed inside, as if I'd just blown up a very pretty big balloon and somebody had stuck a pin into it. I didn't know there was going to be more excitement where we were than where Barry and the fire warden would be.

9

The station wagon had no sooner disappeared and the whirring sound of its motor faded away, leaving us with Barry's orders to go back to bed ringing in our ears, than I remembered the blank sheet of typewriter paper I had in my pocket and which we hadn't bothered to show to Barry.

Little Jim and Tom Till didn't know anything about what was going on, and, being sleepy anyway, they seemed glad to get back to their tent and make a dive back into the sleep from which they had dragged themselves a little while before.

Dragonfly was suspicious, though, and when he noticed Poetry and Big Jim and Circus and me talking together, he got a stubborn expression in his voice and aimed a question at us. "You guys got a secret of some kind?"

We didn't want him to start any fuss. Besides, sometimes he wasn't such a dumb person to let in on a secret. So for a little while we left Little Jim and Tom Till alone in their tent, and the five of us went into the other tent, lit a lantern, unfolded the piece of typewriter paper, and warmed it over the hot top of the lantern.

In only a few minutes we were again looking at a map of the territory. It showed the camp where we were and the place where the little Ostberg girl had been lying, just like the other map we'd found. Also some other places were identified, such as Santa's boathouse, the fire warden's cabin, and the broken twig trail, which led off in different directions.

"Both maps are alike," Circus said, and it looked as if they were.

Poetry traced the faint markings of the new map with his pencil so that we could study it better.

"What do you suppose Bob had two maps for?" Dragonfly asked.

And Poetry answered by saying, "He maybe had only one at first, but when he lost it—the one we found last week—he or his dad made another one."

"Yeah," I said, with a question mark in my voice, "but why draw them in invisible ink?"

"Maybe so nobody would think they were maps."

"But how could Bob *himself* know the different places if he couldn't see the lines and different marks?" I asked, wondering.

It was Dragonfly who answered my doubt by saying, "Oh, he probably had what they call an 'original'—and as soon as he'd memorized it, he drew another one in invisible ink and tore the first one up!"

His idea made sense, I thought and said so, and so did Poetry.

But we weren't getting anywhere—and weren't supposed to, anyway. It certainly didn't seem fair that Barry hadn't let us go with him, but he was camp boss and that was that, and we were supposed to crawl back into our sleeping bags and go to sleep. Imagine that! Right while Barry and the fire warden and maybe the police were capturing old hook-nosed John Till and his son Bob! *Imagine* it! It was terribly disappointing.

And then all of a sudden Dragonfly gasped and said, "Gang! Look!" He was holding up the new map between his dragonflylike eyes and the light. His voice had contagious excitement in it, so we all looked quick to see what he saw. But it wasn't anything—only two crude-looking fish away off on the part of the map that was supposed to represent a lake.

"A couple of fish," I said, disgusted with him for getting us excited over nothing. "That's to show you there is a lake there."

"Yeah," he said, still excited, "but look where they *are!* They're right over there where that island is where we caught our walleyes today."

Big Jim answered by saying, "Maybe they're supposed to locate a good fishing place."

And then Dragonfly got an idea that sent our minds whirling like summer cyclones at Sugar Creek. He said, "You know what that is? That's where the *island* is, and that's where John Till has been catching the big fish to put the ransom money in, and that island's where maybe the rest of the money is right this very minute. I'll bet that's where they'll go to get the rest of it, if Barry or the police don't catch 'em first!"

Well sir, you could have knocked me over with an invisible-ink map when Dragonfly gave us that wonderful idea. It sounded exactly right, and it seemed a shame that I hadn't thought of it first.

In fact, for a minute it almost seemed I had, because all of a sudden I was remembering what I'd thought in the afternoon when Poetry and I had been exploring that island looking for clues. Also I remembered that island was where I'd wanted to go to hunt for treasure in the first place when I'd thought of playing Robinson Crusoe and his man Friday and also *Treasure Island.*

I just knew that Dragonfly and I were right, so as quick as a flash I said, "If we really want to capture Bob and old John Till, we'd better beat it over to that little island and be hiding there somewhere when they get there and capture them ourselves."

Big Jim answered me in a tone of voice that sounded as if he thought I was only about half bright. "Who wants to get the living daylights knocked out of him in the middle of the night? When you saw him the *first* time, didn't he have a big hunting knife?"

I remembered that he had. In fact, in my mind's eye I could still see that wicked-looking knife with its five-inch-long blade that looked as if it could not only make a quick slice into the stomach of a fish but could do the same thing to a boy. When Big Jim said that to me like that, it seemed maybe he was right and that I was very ignorant for wanting to be brave without using good sense.

"Besides," Big Jim said, "those two silly-looking fish on the map don't mean a thing. We'd better all get some sleep, or we'll be as tired as wrung-out dishrags tomorrow."

Well, that was orders, and a boy is supposed to obey anybody who has a right to be his boss, such as a schoolteacher or a camp leader or either one of his parents or somebody he is working for. Big Jim didn't always get obeyed, though, because our gang nearly always voted on important things to decide what to do.

So right away Poetry, who thought my idea wasn't so bad after all, spoke up and said, "I move we all get into Barry's big boat and go roaring over to that island, beach the boat on the sandy shore of the cove behind some willows, and be there waiting when Bob and his dad come—if they do."

"Second the motion," I said quick.

But Big Jim exploded our idea by saying, "It's *Barry's* orders to go to bed."

It certainly wasn't easy to go to bed when there was so much excitement we'd rather be mixed up in, but orders were orders. So pretty soon I was in my sleeping bag in the tent with Dragonfly and Poetry. Big Jim and Circus had decided to go back to Santa's cabin to spend the rest of the night as they'd planned to do in the first place.

Pretty soon, in spite of feeling excited and wondering whether anybody would catch John Till and Bob, I must have dropped off to sleep, not even knowing I was going to do it. A certain poem says, "No boy knows when he goes to sleep." It seemed like even in my sleep I could hear an outboard motor roaring out on the lake, first coming close to us, then fading away, and then a little later coming back again.

Once, when I was half awake and half asleep, I heard Poetry turn over beside me, and then I heard him whisper, "Bill, listen, will you? Somebody's out there in a motorboat going back and forth in front of our dock."

It took a while for me to realize where I was and why, and then I was actually listening to a motorboat out on our lake, sounding as if somebody was doing what Poetry said he was.

Poetry sat up, scrambled over to the tent flap, and worked it open.

In another second I had my red head beside his, and we were both looking out across the moonlit water and seeing a dark, fast-moving boat out there.

"He's crazy!" Poetry said in my left ear, and I said to him in his right one, "He's just cutting big wide circles."

It seemed silly for anybody to do what he was doing. So, because it was a crazy night anyway and so many odd things had happened on our fishing trip, Poetry and I squeezed our way through the tent flap and went down to the dock to see what on earth anybody was doing out there, just going round and round like that.

And then Poetry gasped and said, *"There isn't anybody in that boat. It's empty!"*

Just then the boat came into the middle of a big wide silver path, which lakes have on moonlit nights when you look out across them in the direction of the moon. And I saw that Poetry was right.

I could hardly believe my surprised eyes, but in that silver path was a motorboat about the size of the one Bob Till had gone away in, cutting big, terribly fast wide circles, going round and round and round. The motor sounded exactly like the big black-shrouded one I knew how to run so well and which Bob had taken from Santa's dock.

It didn't make sense—a boat out there without anybody in it.

"It's getting *closer!* The wind is blowing it toward the shore. It gets closer every time it makes a circle!"

What to do or whether to do anything was the question. Poetry and I stood there on the dock in our pajamas, not slapping at the mosquitoes, because when the wind blows, as it was right then, mosquitoes' small wings can't control their flight, and they stop looking for boys to bite.

Whirr! Roar! Whizz! And also *Plop! Plop! Plop!* The motor was doing the whirring and the whizzing, and the bottom of the boat was doing the plopping on the waves.

"It's empty!" we said to each other.

"Maybe whoever was in it fell out. Maybe it was John Till, and he was drunk and fell out, and the boat just keeps on running," I said.

I knew a motorboat could do that. If the steering handle was set, it would maybe stay set, and the motor would keep on going until it ran out of gas or rammed into the shore somewhere.

Then the boat straightened out a little, as though the steering handle had swung around, which they do sometimes when nobody holds onto them. Now it came roaring straight toward our dock at a terrific rate of speed! In another half minute it would crash into the end of the dock where we were, right there by the flagpole. It was coming as straight as a torpedo and almost as fast, I thought, as though this was a war and somebody had fired a torpedo right toward where we were.

And then a second later, while my mind was whirling, not believing it could or would happen, the sharp prow of that big white boat with the fierce racing motor on the other end of it struck with a crash that jarred the dock, glanced sideways, swerved up along its edge, and ran into the sandy shore. At the same time, the propeller, down in the water, struck the shallow sandy bottom, which made the motor tilt forward.

The motor made a couple of discouraged-sounding sneezes and coughs and stopped.

Almost before the sound of the crash had

stopped splitting my eardrums, I was over by the boat, looking down and shining my flashlight into it. There lying in the bottom was a quart-sized whiskey bottle, and my imagination told me that maybe John Till had been in the boat and that he had gotten drunk and had fallen out and was out there in the lake somewhere, already drowned. My heart sank as I thought of what a hurt heart Little Tom Till would have when he found out.

The waves of the lake were splashing against the dock posts and lapping at the shore and the boat, and it was a terribly tense minute.

And then Poetry, who was beside me, grabbed my arm as if he had just heard something terribly important and said, "Listen . . . *sh . . . listen!*"

I listened but didn't hear anything at first. Then all of a sudden I did, and it was a scared voice calling from somewhere, crying, "Help! Help!"

10

I certainly didn't dream that things were going to turn out the way they did when that boat whammed itself into our dock and up onto the shore, turning partway over on its side, and we heard a voice calling from somewhere, "Help! Help! Help!"

The first thing I thought of was that somebody—I didn't know who—was out there drowning and had to have help right away.

Santa's house was several hundred yards up the shore, and any yelling any of us could have done for Big Jim and Circus to come and help us couldn't have been heard by them. And by the time any of us could have run up there and wakened them, it would have been too late to save whoever's life needed to be saved.

Quick as anything, I said to Poetry, "We've got to do something, or maybe somebody will drown out there!"

But I didn't have to tell Poetry to get going. He was the fastest-acting barrel-shaped boy you ever saw. In less time than it takes me to write it for you, Poetry had picked up two oars that were lying there and tossed them into the rowboat that was on the opposite side of the dock and in an instant was unwinding the anchor rope from around the dock post.

Then he yelled to me, "Hurry up and get in and get the oars into the oarlocks, and let's row out quick and save him!"

Even while we were making a lot of noise, I could still hear that voice out there calling, "Help! Help! H–e–l–p!"

We got the boat's prow headed into the waves, which is what you have to do when you row on a lake, or you'll maybe get your boat filled with water.

Then I heard another yell coming from the direction of the tents, and it was Dragonfly racing toward us in flapping pajamas, wanting to know what was going on and why.

I yelled back to him from the boat I was already in and said, "Hey, you—Dragonfly! Beat it down to Santa's cabin and tell Big Jim and Circus to get Santa's motorboat and come out to help us! There's somebody drowning out there in the moonlight!"

As quick as anything, Poetry and I were on our way. Our boat had three life-preserver cushions in it—enough for Poetry and me and whoever was out there, which of course had to be John Till, I thought, on account of the whiskey bottle in the bottom of the boat that had just roared its way up onto our shore.

If our own boat should be upset and we were tossed out into the water, we could swim to our cushions and by keeping our bodies down under the water and holding onto the cushions for dear life, we could manage to keep our faces above water, and the cushions would hold us up.

Poetry and I sat in the middle seat, side by side, with Poetry sitting nearer the center than I, so that the boat would be well balanced, on account of he was a whole lot heavier than I was. Each one of us used an oar, and we rowed as fast as we could in the direction the call for help had come from.

Our oars made squeaking noises in the locks, the blades made a little splashing sound in the water, and the waves plopping against the prow made it hard for us to hear the calls for help and also hard to tell just which direction to go. But we kept on rowing hard, and I could see the shore getting farther and farther away.

I was glad that my parents had taught me how to work on the farm and that I had muscles that sometimes felt as strong as the muscles of the man in a poem Poetry is always quoting, "The Village Blacksmith," which goes:

Under the spreading chestnut tree
The village smithy stands.
The smith—a mighty man is he,
With large and sinewy hands,
And the muscles of his brawny arms
Are strong as iron bands.

But even though my arm muscles felt that strong, my knees felt sort of weak as I realized that a man's life was depending on us. We kept on rowing as hard and as fast as we could, grunting and sweating and hoping and also doing what any boy with good sense, or even without it, would do at a time like that—*praying* as hard as anything.

Anyway *I* was, and I was asking God to please help us get there quick. When a boy is in the middle of such dangerous excitement as I was in, he will ask God to help him, even though he hasn't been a very good boy and isn't sure God will have anything to do with him. All of a sudden I was thinking of Little Tom and his nice mother, and it just seemed it would be terrible for them to lose their dad, even if he was maybe the meanest man that ever lived at Sugar Creek.

Another reason I was praying with every grunt was that I knew John Till wasn't a Christian. And if he didn't become one before he died, he'd never get to go to heaven, because my parents had told me the Bible says, "Unless one is born again he cannot see the kingdom of God." Anybody who knows what Dad calls the "ABC's of the gospel" knows that you can be born again just by letting the Savior into your heart. But John Till had never done that.

I guess maybe I didn't use any words with my prayer, though, but only some worried thoughts, which I sort of shot up to heaven as quick as I could, the way I shoot arrows with my bow when I'm back home. In fact, for a while it seemed I was shooting prayer-arrows up to God and that on the end of each one, instead of a little feather, there was a note on a strip of paper. And on each note I'd written, "Please, heavenly Father, old John Till's soul is lost, and if he drowns without being saved, it'll be terrible. Help us get to him quick."

Then Poetry interrupted my thoughts saying, "Stop rowing a minute and listen!"

I let my oar rest for a moment, and right away the waves made our boat swerve a little, as though it would swing around if we didn't keep on rowing.

But I heard a voice not more than fifty feet farther on. Looking quick, I saw something dark in the water, struggling. And the voice with a desperate gasp cried, "Hurry—I—help!" Then it stopped.

I tell you we hurried then. I kept on sending up prayer-arrows, grunting and pulling and wishing. Then without knowing I was going to say it, I said, "Oh, please don't let him drown. Because Poetry and I have got a secret about one of Your Bible verses that says if two of us agree on something we ask for, You will answer us."

It just seemed that John Till *had* to be saved, on account of it seemed that promise in the Bible was especially about him. Then, again without knowing I was going to say it aloud, I said, "And here comes another arrow with the same thing written on it."

And Poetry said, "What arrow? What are you talking about?"

I explained it to him while we rowed harder.

And even though he didn't say much, I knew he was doing the same thing I was. My parents had taught me to pray when I was little, and I still liked to, even though my folks sometimes might wonder if I ever did or not, because I was sometimes too mischievous. Also sometimes I wasn't always what they called a "good boy," which is an expression they use when they mean I ought to behave myself.

Soon we were close to John Till, and I saw it was really him, and he didn't have any life preserver. He had probably been drunk and had just tumbled out of his boat while it was racing terribly fast, and he had been swimming ever since.

I quick grabbed up the cushion in front of my feet and with a wide sweep of my arm tossed it out toward him. My aim was as good as David's had been when he had used his sling-shot on the giant that time in the Bible.

The pillow landed *ker-plop* right in front of old John, and I saw him make a desperate lunge toward it and grab hold with both arms. Then I heard him yell in a sputtering voice something I never dreamed I'd hear from old John Till that night. It was "Thank God, I'm saved!"

Then he quit trying to swim and just lay back and held onto the cushion and let himself float, with only his face above water and the cushion in front of his chin. That is the way to float, if you ever have to hold onto a life-preserver cushion.

In a moment we had our boat there, and old John was crying and gasping and saying, "Thank God—oh, thank you, boys, thank you!"

How to get him into the boat was the question, though, for the minute he would try to get in, his heavy weight might tip us over. But in spite of being exhausted and gasping for breath, John Till still had good sense. He didn't try to climb in right away but got his breath first.

Besides, in a minute Circus and Big Jim, with Dragonfly holding a flashlight to help them see us, came motoring out. In a little while we had John in the boat, and we were all on our way to shore, with John so tired out he just laid down his terribly wet self and sort of shook and sniffled and half cried while we moved along.

I tell you, it's a wonderful feeling when you've done something like that. You're glad not only because you helped do it, but, if you believe what Poetry and I believed, you feel as though you and the heavenly Father are very good friends—which is maybe the best feeling a boy ever has.

As we rowed along toward shore, John Till just lay in the bottom of the boat like a terribly big fish that had just been caught and was so tired out he couldn't move.

Pretty soon, Poetry whispered, "Do you think he's pretending to be good, and that he just said those religious words back there to fool us and is maybe playing possum? Do you think when we get to shore he'll quick make a dive for the bushes and run away?"

I'd seen possums act like that. They were lively until they were caught; then they would do what is called "play possum"—just roll over on their sides and curl up into a half circle and shut their eyes and act dead until we or the dogs went away a few yards. Then they would come to life quick, scramble to their ridiculous feet, which look like hands, and run to a tree and climb up it or to a hole in the ground and dive into it.

"I don't know," I said to Poetry, "but he sounded like he meant what he said when he said those words back there." I wanted to believe it, because I wanted Tom Till to have a brand-new dad like Circus had gotten when *his* pop had been saved a couple of years before.

Well, it turned out that I was right. That whiskey bottle we'd seen in the bottom of his boat hadn't had whiskey in it at all but was one Little Jim had put a gospel tract in! Old John had found it and read it, and the Lord Himself had used it to do what our Sugar Creek minister calls "convict him of his sins." On top of that, he had stopped to read the message in the other whiskey bottle, the one that had been used as a marker for a good crappie-fishing place out in front of the Indian cemetery. Also he had been listening on his little radio to the program of The Church of the Cross.

So, after he had accidentally tumbled out of the boat tonight, he'd gotten half scared to death, and all the verses of the Bible and the sermons he had heard came splashing into his mind. And without stopping to think that he didn't believe in God, he had prayed to Him to not only save his body from drowning but to save his soul from being lost.

When we rescued him, he had the other $5,000 of the ransom money in his trousers pocket. It was pretty wet but was as good as gold. And do you know what? He told us he hadn't been helping the real kidnapper at all but had only wanted to get the $1,000 reward for finding the missing money.

"And now, boys," John's gruff, trembling voice said, as we listened to him explain things, "you'll have to start praying for Bob. We had a quarrel tonight, and he's gone away somewhere."

"Where?" Tom asked.

All of us were sitting around a campfire, which we'd started quick to get John warmed up after we'd got some of Barry's dry clothes on him and a blanket wrapped around him. Most of the rest of us were wrapped in blankets, too.

John looked down at his red-haired, freckle-faced, trembling-voiced boy and said, "I don't know. I—he thought we ought to keep the $5,000 instead of turning it in. I—I'm afraid I was too hard on him, maybe. But when we couldn't agree about this $5,000, I took the boat and left him there at the Indian cemetery."

We asked old John different questions, one

of them being, "How'd you know where the ransom money was?"

And he said, "I studied the newspapers and the pictures, and I found the kidnapper's map in the grave house of an old Indian chief. I made two copies in invisible ink—one for myself and the other for Bob. But I lost mine somewhere, and you boys found it."

"But why, if you only wanted the thousand-dollar reward, did you bury the money in the fish in the icehouse?" we asked him.

"I didn't," he said, just as Tom shoved a stick into the fire and about a thousand yellow sparks shot in different directions up toward the sky. "The kidnapper buried it there. I'd been digging it up. I had five thousand dollars already dug up and was coming back to get the rest of it, but you boys beat me to it. Then when I went into the icehouse, you slammed the door on me and barred it, and I would have stayed there until the police came, but Bob, who had just gotten up here, heard me hollering and let me out."

Poetry spoke up and said, with doubt in his voice, "But if you were only after the money so you could get the reward for finding it, why did you run away?"

"I was afraid the police wouldn't believe my story."

Well, there is the whole mystery untangled for you, and a wonderful camping trip was all over. Boy oh boy, I hope I get to go again next year—if not to the same place, then up to

Canada or somewhere where there will be even more exciting adventures than there were this year.

But before that happens there'll be a whole year full of different things that will happen back home at Sugar Creek. I just know that something terribly interesting *will* happen to us before another summer rolls around.

In fact, there was a letter from my folks in our mailbox at the dock the very day we left camp, saying, "We'll be looking for you, Bill, and do we ever have interesting news for you! Don't try to guess what it is, because you can't."

And, well, all the way home in our station wagon, I did just what my parents told me not to—I kept trying to guess what the interesting news would be.

The Original Sugar Creek Series:

The New Sugar Creek Gang Series

The New Sugar Creek Gang #1

When he and his family move to the neighborhood surrounding Sugar Creek, 11-year old Les decides to explore where all those exciting old adventures happened. But by that night, Les is caught up in a mystery of his own.

ISBN#0-8024-8661-4

The New Sugar Creek Gang #2

After Les and Bits's church is set on fire, one of the Sugar Creek Gang starts acting awfully suspicious. Worst off all, a one-of-a-kind bike places the Sugar Creeker at the scene of the crime! Now it's up to the new Sugar Creek Gang to find a way to stand by their friend - and to solve the mystery before its too late!
ISBN#0-8024-8662-2

The New Sugar Creek Gang #3

When turkeys, deer and other creatures around Sugar Creek begin to turn up wounded, rumor has it wolves are to blame. Worried about the injured animals and their human neighbors, the New Sugar Creek Gang vows to get to the bottom of the mystery.

ISBN# 0-8024-3178-X

The New Sugar Creek Gang #4

After Lynn wins a dinosaur-drawing contest, the New Sugar Creek Gang gets to join a real, honest-to-goodness dinosaur dig in Arizona! When important items start disappearing from the site, it looks like the kids may be sent home unless the gang can solve the mystery and save the day!

ISBN# 0-8024-8664-9